NIGHTMARES!
HOW WILL YOURS END?

CASTLE OF HORROR

By Don Wulffson

An RGA Book

PRICE STERN SLOAN
Los Angeles

Copyright © 1995 RGA Publishing Group, Inc.
Published by Price Stern Sloan, Inc.,
A member of The Putnam & Grosset Group,
New York, New York.

ISBN 0-8431-3862-9
First Edition
10 9 8 7 6 5 4 3 2 1

Library of Congress Cataloging-in-Publication Data

Wulffson, Don L.
    Castle of horror / written by Don L. Wulffson.
        p. cm. — (Nightmares! How will yours end?)
    Summary: The reader's decisions control the outcome of a stay in a nightmarish castle in Scotland.
    ISBN 0-8431-3862-9
    1. Plot-your-own stories. [1. Castles—Fiction. 2. Plot-your-own stories.] I. Title. II. Series: Wulffson, Don L. Nightmares! How will yours end?
    PZ7.W96373Cas 1995
    [Fic]—dc20   94-29371
                                                                      CIP
                                                                       AC

COVER AND INTERIOR ICON ILLUSTRATIONS BY DOMINICK DOMINGO.

For my daughters, Jennifer and Gwendolyn, with love.
—D. W.

HOW TO FIND OUT HOW YOUR NIGHTMARE WILL END

Try to stay awake—you won't want to miss any of the exciting endings in *Castle of Horror*. Most of them are nightmarish . . . but if you're lucky, you'll pick the right route and find your way back to reality. Should you take the Giver of Wishes' offer to make you live forever, or will you follow the seemingly endless corridor before you? Will you hide in the forest from the oncoming soldiers, or wade through the mysterious multicolored stream to escape from them? The choice is yours. Here's how it works:

First turn to the next page and learn where your nightmare takes place. Read on and find out which friends will be joining you. Then begin your adventure. Your quest is to find a way out of the Castle of Horror and back to your Aunt Cora's house in Devon, England, where you and your father are staying.

It's easy, it's fun, and it's very, very scary. Just read to the end of each section and follow the directions. You will be offered a choice of pages to turn to, or instructed to simply go to the next page. And what happens when you reach the ending of one story? Just go back to the beginning, try making a different decision, and take a whole new frightening route!

Ready to begin? Good luck . . . and **SWEET DREAMS!**

THE SETTING

You and your father are staying with your Aunt Cora and your two cousins, Rodney and Elise, at their home in Devon, England. Nearby are the ruins of the historical Ormonde Castle, which your cousins had shown you earlier in the day. Tonight, exhausted from jet lag and the day's events, you drift to sleep with the castle's history of murder and sorcery that Rodney had told you fresh in your mind. But you wouldn't have closed your eyes at all if you had known about the horrible nightmare that lies ahead of you.

Your nightmare is set in eerie Ormonde Castle. Once you enter its sodden walls, you realize that the ruins are now completely restored. You, Rodney, and Elise meet in the dark, ghostly hallways of the castle. Cold and confused as you try to follow the torches' light in front of you, your fear increases when you realize that the castle's guards are chasing you—and will stop at nothing short of your death to ensure your capture. You squeeze through crawl spaces, race down corridors, climb creaky stairwells, and enter magical rooms with spell-casting sorcerers—all in a desperate attempt to get away from the soldiers and back to your Aunt Cora's house. There are rotten-smelling corpses and creepy creatures of all forms and sizes whose only goal, it seems, is to terrify you.

Beyond the castle walls, streams, pathways, people, and animals can transform in front of you, leaving you at a loss as to where to turn and what to do. Any number of unexpected events may occur, for this medieval setting contains the Castle of Horror, and it is highly changeable, completely unfamiliar, and totally unpredictable.

CAST OF CHARACTERS

ELISE CULLEN, 14, is your brave and adventurous cousin who has long, auburn hair that fits her fireball personality. Although she is brash at times, she has a warm heart and is devoted to her family and friends.

RODNEY CULLEN, 13, is Elise's brother. He is more cautious than his sister and has a tendency to be somewhat pessimistic. Sometimes he can be a little impatient, but he is quick-witted and bright and you get along well with him.

AUNT CORA, your father's sister, is in a wheelchair due to an accident that happened a long time ago. Her smile and understanding nature have always made her one of your favorite relatives, and her capacity for comforting others makes her a wonderful mother substitute while you are so far from home.

YOUR FATHER, the strong, silent type, has taken this trip with you for two reasons: to get closer to you, and to give your mom some time to herself to finish her novel. He is close to his sister, Cora, whom he grew up with in England. She stayed, but he left for the United States to go to college, and several years later he met your mom. Everyone says you look exactly like your dad and nothing like your mother.

Giving your mother some time alone to write her novel, you and your dad are visiting your British relatives, the Cullens, who live in the town of Devon, England. Your Aunt Cora, in a wheelchair from a bad fall years ago, always seems to have a warm smile and a good word to say to everyone. Your 14-year-old cousin, Elise, is spirited and cheerful with a taste for adventure. Your other cousin, Rodney, 13, is the opposite of Elise. He is nervous, moody, and has a tendency to see the downside of everything.

You spend your first morning with your dad, Aunt Cora, Rodney, and Elise, taking a tour of Devon. That afternoon, at the suggestion of Aunt Cora, you and your cousins walk up the coast to the ruins of Ormonde Castle, three miles away. Built in the 14th century on a low, rocky bluff overlooking the sea, Ormonde is now little more than a dark, eerie ruin. It is roofless, and most of the walls have collapsed into piles of rubble. Walking around through the heaps of ancient stone blackened from centuries of foul weather, Rodney takes pleasure in relating some of the gory details of beheadings, sorcery, murder, plagues, and wars that are part of the castle's bloody history.

That night you return to the Cullen home, and after supper, you and your cousins watch the "telly,"

Turn to the next page.

as they call it. But you are worn out from the day's events, and British television—at least the humor—takes some getting used to, so you turn in early. Uneasy in the unfamiliar house and bed, and bothered by your visit to Ormonde Castle, you are having a hard time falling asleep. All the ugly stories your cousin Rodney told you about the place aren't helping, either.

As an old clock ticks beside your bed, you hear the others head off to their rooms. Aunt Cora sleeps downstairs. Elise has her own small bedroom, also downstairs, and since Rodney has a tendency to snore, your dad has volunteered to sleep with Rodney in his room upstairs, down the hall from yours.

The house grows silent. Though your head is filled with dark, creepy thoughts, exhaustion finally overtakes you, and you fall into a troubled sleep.

Cold and alone, in loose-fitting clothes and sandals, you are in a dream that places you walking within the walls of Ormonde Castle. But the place is not in ruins as you saw it. Now it is standing and in good shape. It looks as though it has been recently completed—almost as if you were back in the 14th century!

"I'm dreaming!" a voice inside your head insists. But are you? Everything seems so real. Along a wall, numerous torches are burning. They fill the air with

Turn to the next page.

smoke, and the flickering light dances, creating macabre shadows. From a candlelit room, you hear laughter . . . and then a scream. Atop a wall, metallic silhouettes of men in armor are running in the direction of the scream.

"Cousin, is that you?" someone with a familiar voice whispers.

You turn around to see Elise and Rodney, dressed similarly to you, emerging from behind the rounded stone wall of a turret.

"How did we get here?" whispers Rodney, his eyes wide as he looks around at the dark, ominous walls that enclose the main courtyard of the castle.

"I think I'm having a dream," you tell him, "or a nightmare."

"Then wake up!" says Elise, shaking you. "I don't want to be in your stupid nightmare."

"I can't," you tell her. "Do you think I want to be here any more than you do?"

"Then how are we all going to get out of here?" moans Rodney.

"I don't know," you answer, looking all around. "Maybe somewhere in the castle there's a way out. Maybe if we—?"

"Who goes there?" a harsh, booming voice suddenly demands.

Turn to the next page.

In terror, you and your cousins spot a man in flowing robes, holding a lighted torch in his hand and looking down from a balcony. You see that the right side of his face is horribly scarred, and the socket of his right eye is nothing more than an empty hole.

"Halt!" he bellows. Then he is on the move, hurrying down from above. Soldiers are on his heels, as he rushes across the courtyard.

Not wanting to confront him *or* his troops, the three of you run through an open doorway. Inside to your left, is a dark, winding stairwell leading up into the castle. Dashing to it, you find that the stairwell not only leads up, but also down . . . into the castle's shadowy depths.

"Up or down?" Elise asks.

You hesitate.

"Decide!" demands Rodney.

If you choose to go up the stairs,
*turn to the **next page**.*

If you choose to go down the stairs,
*turn to **page 66**.*

"Head up the stairs!" you shout to Elise and Rodney. But they are already taking the winding, narrow steps two at a time.

As the three of you climb, the winding stairwell becomes narrower and darker. Hardly able to see your feet, not to mention what's ahead, you feel your way along with your hands against the cold stone walls.

"Faster!" cries Elise. But you and your cousins are already tripping and falling against each other as you frantically clamber up the stairs.

"I can't go any—" you begin. And then you hear heavy footfalls close behind. "They've followed us up the stairs!" you yell fearfully, as echoing voices boom at you and the smoky light of the torches eerily plays on the walls.

Suddenly Rodney, who was in the lead, stops dead in his tracks. "We can't go up!" he yells. "These stairs lead to a blank wall!"

Struck with terror, the three of you stare in disbelief. Then just as you are about to give up, your terror turns to amazement. A white, glowing door has taken shape in the wall. You pull the attached ring-bolt, and as the door opens, the three of you scramble into a room.

"Close the door!" you scream.

Seconds before the one-eyed, scarred man gets

*Turn to the **next** page.*

you with his upraised dagger, Elise slams the door in his face. As the door closes, it disappears.

"Wow!" you all gasp in unison.

"Welcome," says a voice from the gloomy interior of the room.

You turn around and find an old, wizened little man sitting on a plush purple velvet cushion. In a silver chandelier, three purple candles burn with purple flames. The walls, too, are purple. The place looks pleasant enough, but you still look for an escape route. Nowhere can you see a door or window of any kind.

"Where did the door go?" you ask nervously. "Where are we?"

"In the Wishing Room," the little man says simply. "And I am the Giver of Wishes." His face wrinkles into a smile. "But you may have only one of two."

"What do you mean?" Rodney asks suspiciously.

"You may wish simply to leave, or you may wish to live forever, and *then* leave."

Looking bored, the little man plucks a gold key from the air with his left hand and snaps the fingers of his right. A luminous white door instantly appears. "Now, what do each of you wish?"

"We want to get out of here," Rodney and Elise whine together.

Turn to the next page.

You are not sure—something just doesn't seem right. Not waiting for your answer, the Giver of Wishes tosses the key to Elise. It floats gracefully into her hand. Elise grasps the key and unlocks the door. When she pushes it open, light floods into the room.

"There's a corridor," she says to Rodney, "and it looks empty." Then she turns to you. "Well, are you coming with us?" she asks.

"It's so long I can't even see the end of it," you tell her, looking over Elise's shoulder at the corridor. "I don't know what to do."

If you simply leave with your cousins,
turn to the next page.

If you decide to live forever, and
then leave, turn to page 17.

——"Living forever is tempting," you tell the wrinkled little man, "but like my cousins, I'd just like to leave."

"As you wish," he replies.

And with that, the three of you leave the strange purple room and the even stranger little man. Flaming torches set in iron brackets fixed to the wall illuminate your way down the empty corridor.

As you noticed earlier, the corridor is terribly long. You are beginning to think it goes on forever, when three doors finally come into view. One door is ordinary in shape, but hardly big enough to crawl through. Another is of normal size but an odd oval shape. The third door is painted red and would be normal except for the fact that it is high up on the wall—a good ten or fifteen feet above the floor. There are no stairs leading up to the red door, but on the floor is a ladder that looks long enough to reach it.

"Which door should we try?" you wonder out loud.

"It's up to you," says Elise.

"Yeah, it's your nightmare," adds Rodney, "not ours."

If you open the oval door,
turn to **page 19.**

If you open the small door,
turn to **page 24.**

If you decide on the red door up
on the wall, turn to **page 30.**

"Well, sir," you say, "I guess I'd like to live forever, then leave. It would be great to know you were never going to die."

In the flickering purple glow of the room, an evil smile unfolds on the man's wrinkled face. He points his right hand at you, and instantly his arm transforms into a razor-sharp sword. Paralyzed with terror, you watch as he takes a single swipe at your head. Then you hear Elise and Rodney scream.

Oddly there isn't any pain, but it really makes you dizzy to have your head bouncing up and down on the floor. You swivel your eyes toward your cousins, then at the Giver of Wishes, and then at your own headless body. It is stumbling blindly around the room, banging into things.

"My body!" you scream at the man. "Put me back on my body!"

Cackling laughter is his only response.

Weeping, Elise stops your body from running around frantically and tightly holds on to it.

"Don't forget the head!" screeches the evil man, his sword changing back into an arm as he sits down on his purple cushion.

Ashen faced, Rodney bends down and picks up your head. Elise, walking hand in hand with your headless body, approaches him.

Turn to the next page.

Your eyes swivel toward the Giver of Wishes. "Please," you beg the horrible little man, "please put me back the way I was!"

But the man shakes his head. "Sorry. You made the wrong choice—to live forever." He laughed. "Maybe next time you won't lose your head and be so greedy!"

"Guess I'll go for this one," you say, pulling open the oval-shaped door to what appears to be a storage room. Cautiously the three of you enter.

You are immediately greeted by the delicious aromas of several kinds of cooked food, and farther ahead you can see what appears to be a large kitchen. Beyond that, in shadows, rests a large wooden cage. You can't see what's inside, but you hear plaintive, little whimpering noises coming from it.

Tentatively, hiding behind stacks and barrels of foodstuffs as you go, you make your way toward the large kitchen where several men and women are busily working. In a blackened kettle suspended on iron hooks in a great stone fireplace, a stew of some sort bubbles. At a large wooden chopping block, a butcher and his helper are hacking and slicing meat. Nearby a woman is seated on a stool, kneading dough, then rolling it flat with a long wooden rolling pin. Although you can't see her face, she looks oddly familiar.

Suddenly from behind some potato barrel comes a scrawny, long-limbed man. He is pushing a rickety wooden wheelbarrow with a huge bag of flour precariously balanced in it. Seeing you he is startled and overturns the wheelbarrow.

"Now look what you made me do," the scrawny man says, shaking his head at the spilled bag of flour.

Turn to the next page.

"Sorry, sir," Elise replies before you have a chance to clamp your hand over her mouth.

But it is too late. Every head in the kitchen turns toward you. That's when you realize why the baker looked so familiar. She is your Aunt Cora!

"Mummy!" Rodney and Elise yell, running up to the baker.

The woman cocks her head, and her features wrinkle up in puzzlement. "I ain't your mum."

"But . . . but," says Elise, "you look just like—"

She stops herself as the woman twists her body from the stool, gathers up two heavy wooden crutches and slowly, painfully, makes her way toward the three of you on legs that look almost boneless.

"Aunt Cora," you begin. "What's happened to your—"

"Never laid eyes on you before, child," says the woman. "And me name ain't Cora. 'Tis Maude."

You turn to your cousins. "Maybe it's like reincarnation," you tell them. "Some people say we keep coming back—that we all had past lives and keep returning throughout the centuries as different people and . . ."

You stop what you're saying, your attention diverted as servants wearing leather aprons fling open the door and enter the kitchen bearing round trays

Turn to the next page.

with greasy wood bowls and iron spoons on top. Before the door is closed again, you catch a glimpse of a fancy dining room with several noblemen and noblewomen in ornate clothing seated at a long table.

"They be wantin' more bread," says one of the servants, a round little man with large jowls and a bulbous nose.

"An' more goat's milk," says a messy, wild-haired woman, carrying heavy earthenware pitchers in both hands.

"And for supper," says a tall, balding servant with red cheeks, "the numskull little prince has ordered meat pie, the *special* meat pie."

"Will the little beasty never tire o' that?" the butcher asks, sighing. His eyes drift in the direction of the cage. "Bothers me to be makin' that 'orrible pie for the little swine, day in an' day out."

For a moment your gaze also drifts in the direction of the cage. From the shadows, the whites of some creature's eyes peer out at you. But the corner is too dark for you to see what kind of creature it is.

"An'," says the cook, " 'tis so little in the larder." He dips an iron ladle into the bubbling pot, then slurps a bit of the stewlike mess. As he chews and samples his own cooking, his eyes are on you and your cousins.

Turn to the next page.

And so are the eyes of the baker and the butcher. The other servants, though, look nervously at each other.

"What's going on?" Elise whispers to you.

"We've got to get out here!" hisses Rodney.

Seeing that you are nervous, Maude holds some fruit. "Are you hungry, little darlings?" she asks. "Do you fancy a bite to eat?"

"Oh, no, thank you," says Elise. "We don't want to put you to any trouble. You're busy so we'll just be on our way."

" 'Tis no trouble at all, deary," answers Maude, creaking on her crutches toward Elise.

The butcher, a burly man with a gray beard, puts his hand on your shoulder. He gently pinches your arm. "My, what a healthy young child you are!"

Your eyes roll upward and you find yourself looking into his greasy gray beard. Then you look toward the baker with your Aunt Cora's face. She is laughing heartily as she pats Elise on the head with a beefy hand.

Elise twirls and tries to make a run for it.

Almost in the same instant, you slither out of the butcher's grasp, and Rodney head-butts the cook, who falls in the process and spills a ladleful of hot stew on himself.

Turn to the next page.

But your bid for freedom is short-lived. Servants quickly pounce on the three of you and drag you kicking and screaming toward the large wooden cage. The eyes—which you now see are human—watch you and your cousins struggle. And when you are finally thrown inside the cage you can see that they belong to a scrawny little boy.

Swearing and fuming, the stew-covered cook slams the door shut and bolts it. "That'll hold ya till I'm ready," he says gruffly and walks off.

"What are they going to do to us?" you ask the scrawny boy huddled in the corner of the cage, your heart pounding. But before he answers, you already know the horrible truth.

"Fatten you up," says the boy, sadly resigned to his fate. "And then make meat pies out of you."

You stoop over and examine the small door.

"Looks no bigger than a cabinet," Elise observes.

"Well, it's worth a try," you say, getting down on your knees and pulling it open.

The three of you crawl through the doorway and land on some wooden stairs leading up. Because the stairwell is so low and confining, you find yourself having to walk bent over to climb them. Gradually, as you ascend, the stairwell widens to normal size. Reaching the top, you enter a large gallery, brightly lit by dozens of candles. On the walls are many paintings. Most look freshly painted, and all look rather odd, consisting of strange designs and peculiar interlocking geometric shapes. Studying one of the pictures, you notice it seems to change right before your eyes. In the center where there was once a cat and a woman, you now see a dog and a man. Peering closer to see if there are other things concealed in the picture, you notice the colors begin to swim in circles. And where the man and dog had been there is now a waterfall. It looks incredibly real, as though the glistening torrent is actually spilling over rocks and collecting in a large, gray-blue pond at the base. Strangest of all, it seems as though you can almost *hear* the sound of the cascading falls, too.

"These paintings are amazing!" exclaims Rodney.

Turn to the next page.

Elise shakes her head in disagreement. "They're spooky, if you ask me. They—"

All of you turn at the sound of approaching footsteps. Through an open doorway emerges a woman wearing a paint-spattered smock, velvet slippers, and an embroidered green cap.

"Oh my, and who might you be?" she asks.

You tell her your names.

"And I am Gwendolyn," says the woman. "Please do have a seat, my dears," she says, clearing a sofa.

You and Rodney sit down, but Elise walks over to the odd paintings. "Did you paint all these?" she asks.

"Indeed, I did," replies Gwendolyn with a smile. She sets a fresh canvas on an easel and rummages around in a box filled with paints and brushes. "Do you like them?"

The three of you nod vigorously, afraid of hurting her feelings, but also because the paintings are truly amazing.

"Why, thank you," says Gwendolyn, spreading paints on a palette. "By the way, I've heard that three strangers are within our walls and the soldiers are looking for them." She raises her eyebrows. "I assume from the looks of you that—"

"You're not going to turn us in, are you?" Rodney blurts out.

Turn to the next page.

"Certainly not," she says, beginning to apply paint to the canvas. "But I would like to know what brings you to Ormonde."

"I'm having a nightmare," you explain, sitting forward on the edge of the sofa. "And all we want to do is get out of it. But we don't know how."

"Oh my, you *are* in a pickle!" she replies, continuing to work.

"Gwendolyn," asks Elise, sitting between you and Rodney on the couch, "what are you working on?"

"A picture of many things," she answers, "including the three of you."

"Cool," says Rodney. "When do we get to see it?"

Gwendolyn smiles cryptically, then winks. "Not until you return home. Now if you will kindly describe your home to me."

Rodney pokes you in the ribs. "She's painting us out of this nightmare," he whispers excitedly. "She's painting us back home!"

Gwendolyn continues to paint as Elise describes their home in Devon in great detail. As she concentrates on her work, a change slowly comes over Gwendolyn. Her expression becomes much harder; her eyes narrow and darken. Your heart begins to beat more rapidly. Is it your imagination, or is there some-

Turn to the next page.

thing sinister about the woman?

Then she smiles and you relax. Dismissing your frightened thoughts for a moment, you settle back against the sofa's plush cushions. Suddenly you feel drowsy. Your eyes droop and you feel yourself drifting . . . drifting . . .

You awaken with a start—and stare in disbelief. You're in bed, back in Aunt Cora's house! Greatly relieved you roll over and are about to go back to sleep when you notice in the predawn light a painting on the wall—one that hadn't been there before. It can't be—but it *has* to be. It's the painting that Gwendolyn had been working on in your nightmare.

Stumbling from bed, you switch on a light and make your way to the painting. At first it seems to be a formless collage of shapes and colors. But, in the center of it, a house takes form—Aunt Cora's house, exquisitely detailed. Across from the house is a man in medieval garb standing in the moonlight. Oddly, as detailed as everything else seems to be, the man has no face. It is no more than a white oval.

Slowly the man shrinks and recedes into the painting. Within seconds he has vanished altogether, and a new form emerges. It is a long dagger.

You step forward peering closely at the thing, but already the picture is transforming yet again. Colors

Turn to the next page.

bleed together until the man reappears—this time with a face.

"No!" you gasp, as you recognize the one-eyed man who chased you in your dream, the man whose face was so hideously scarred. In his hand is a dagger, and he is entering your aunt's house. As if it were a camera, the painting follows the man as he moves across a downstairs room, then begins to climb the stairs.

Terror gripping your heart, you back away, stumble against the bed, and sit numbly on the edge, your eyes glued to the painting. With your breath coming in shallow gasps, your mouth is dry and your own throat seems to be strangling you. The painting has you in its power. You cannot speak; you cannot run; you can only sit and watch as the painting changes again and again. Now it has become the picture of a body, your *own* body, lying on a floor . . . in a pool of blood.

You are about to scream when the painting flashes, then turns white.

Leave! you hear your own voice scream within your head. Move! Get out of the room!

Struggling to break your paralyzing fear, you press down on the bed trying to rise. As you do, you see a hand—*your* hand—in the picture pressing

Turn to the next page.

down on a bed. Then as though the painting were a mirror, you see yourself seated in the picture on the bed in the same bedroom you are in! Your face is contorted, twisted by unspeakable horror.

And then you hear a *click*. Is it coming from the painting or from the door behind you?

Then all at once you know the horrible answer. It is coming from both. Now the door in the painting *and* in the room is opening. The scarred man is entering. Silently, with an evil grin, he approaches the seated figure in the painting . . . from the back. You are afraid to turn around—afraid to look at the painting, afraid not to.

There is a glint of steel as a dagger is upraised. And as the dagger in the painting plunges downward, you see and *feel* your eyes go wide with horror. The world spins and goes black.

"Let's check out the red door," you tell your cousins, picking up the ladder and setting it in place against the wall.

"I don't know," says Rodney. "That ladder doesn't look very sturdy."

He is about to continue protesting, when suddenly the three of you freeze. Down the corridor, voices and footsteps are coming closer. Then, around a bend, dark shadows stretch into view.

Rodney gasps and is the first up the ladder. Elise is close behind. You steady the ladder for them, and watch as Rodney opens the red door. Once he and Elise have crawled through, you begin to climb up.

But panic grips your heart as the shadows coming around the bend materialize into soldiers.

"Halt!" yells one.

You start to scramble up faster . . . and then the rungs of the ladder begin to crack as you step on them.

"Hurry!" Elise cries, peering wide-eyed down at you.

Your heart is beating like a jackhammer as you frantically scurry up the ladder. Just as it breaks up completely into nothing more than a pile of sticks, Rodney and Elise grab you and pull you through the door.

Turn to the next page.

"Thanks!" you gasp, and then you see the fear in your cousins' eyes. You look behind you. The soldiers are practically upon you . . . and they have their own ladder.

"Slam the door!" you shout. Together the three of you push the heavy door closed and latch it just as the soldiers start climbing their ladder.

"That was too close for me!" you gasp, as you listen to the soldiers curse angrily from the other side of the door.

Turning around, you face a long hallway. While running down it, you pass a door that is slightly ajar.

"In here!" you yell, pushing open the heavy door and rushing inside with Rodney and Elise right behind you.

The three of you find yourselves in a large room. Softly shutting the door, you hope the soldiers won't find you. Still, you have to be prepared. You step into the room and look around for places to hide and possible escape routes. Against one wall is a large, upright wardrobe; on another is a narrow window without glass. On a third wall is a closed door. Next to that is a stone stairwell leading upward.

Tentatively, Rodney moves toward the door, while Elise's eyes are fixed on the stairs.

You look from the wardrobe to the window to the

Turn to the next page.

door, and finally to the stairs. Which way should you go? Suddenly the head of an ax bursts through the door you just entered. The wood cracks, then splits, and another blow makes a large hole. A hand in a black leather glove with iron studs around its wrist plunges through and feels for the latch. You have to make a decision—*now!*

If you choose the wardrobe,
turn to the next page.

If you choose the window,
turn to page 36.

If you choose the stairs,
turn to page 54.

If you choose the door,
turn to page 112.

Rodney and Elise run toward the window, but the nearest thing to you is the wardrobe, so you duck into it. Petrified, you peer out through a crack in its door.

You see Rodney and Elise scrambling through the window just as strong arms grab hold of them. You want to help them, but there is nothing you can do.

"Wha-what are you going to do with us?" stammers Rodney.

"Off with his face!" laughs an ugly soldier with long, greasy hair.

That's weird, you think. Isn't it supposed to be "Off with his head"?

The soldier raises a strange little sword that looks like a toy over his head.

"Nooo!" Rodney cries.

The sword swipes downward . . . and Rodney's face falls to the floor with a plop, lying there like a mask.

"What did you do to my brother, you jerks?" Elise yells.

Oddly there is no blood from either the face on the floor or Rodney's faceless head. He does not even seem to be in any pain. He just stands there, faceless, scratching his head as though he were puzzled.

"Where's the third one of ya?" the soldier demands of Elise.

Turn to the next page.

You are about to come out of your hiding place to help save her. Elise, too terrified to speak, backs away as the soldier lifts his toylike sword again.

Lifting her hand to cover her face, she is horrified when the sword swoops down and cuts it off. As she stares wide-eyed at her hand on the floor, you are amazed again at the absence of blood.

"Where's your friend?" the soldier demands.

Suddenly the disconnected hand rises, floating across the room toward you and pointing at the closet. When the hand reaches the door you are hiding behind, its fingers close around the knob and begin to turn it.

As the door swings open flooding the wardrobe with light, you scream.

Then your eyes adjust.

"What's wrong?" asks your father, alarmed by your scream. "And what are you doing in there?"

You blink and look around. You are in the closet in the upstairs bedroom of Aunt Cora's house. Your father, in his pajamas, is standing in front of you, his hand still on the closet door. Elise and Rodney peer into the room with concerned looks on their faces.

"I was having a nightmare," you try to explain, in a flood of fear, confusion, embarrassment—and relief. "But how," you ask groggily, "did I end up in here?"

Turn to the next page.

"Well, kiddo," says your dad, "looks to me like you were sleepwalking." He reaches out and takes your hand. "Now, how about coming out of there?"

Now more embarrassed than anything else, you step from the closet and thankfully out of your nightmare.

"Quick! Out the window!" you yell, climbing out the narrow opening and dropping down to a tile-covered rooftop. Your cousins on your heels, you race across the roof through the moonlit night. A voice yells at you from behind, then an arrow whizzes by and skitters off the tile.

Reaching the end of the roof, you climb onto the rampart behind the fortress wall. The three of you edge along it, then run down stone steps into the main courtyard. You duck into a dark alleyway, just as the soldiers run past searching for you.

Across the way, set in the fortress wall, is a large wooden gate.

"If we can make it to that gate, maybe we can get out of this miserable castle," Elise says. "I say we make a run for it."

"It's too dangerous," warns Rodney. "Let's just hide here in the alley. Maybe they'll give up looking for us."

Both of your cousins turn to you. "What do you think?" they ask in unison.

If you run to the door in the gate,
turn to the next page.

If you continue hiding in the alley,
turn to page 43.

"You wait here," you tell your cousins. "I'll go check out the gate."

Across the courtyard, picking your way from house to house and from shadow to shadow, you sneak to the gate. You pull an iron latch; the gate swings open. You wave your cousins over.

Moments later the three of you are outside the castle walls running through a wooded area, then out across a meadow. You keep glancing back, happy to see that no one is following.

"We made it!" you pant, slowing your pace to a walk.

The sky darkens and high clouds, backlit in yellow by a full moon, fill the sky. As the meadow slopes down into a valley, ground fog swirls at your feet, whipped about by a frigid wind. The cold pierces your thin clothing. You are chilled to the bone. It begins to drizzle, and you look for shelter. Then the sky opens up and it pours. Still unable to find cover, you trudge on and are soon soaked to the skin.

"Boy, am I freezing," Rodney says, shaking from head to toe.

"*Brrrr!*" Elise exclaims, hugging herself for warmth. "So am I."

You are also cold but say nothing. You just keep walking, numb with exhaustion.

Turn to the next page.

Ahead through the curtain of rain you spot a small cottage. Sweet-smelling smoke drifts from its chimney, and light flickers from within. A form of some kind, candle in hand, is at a window peering out.

"Let's head for it," you say. "Maybe whoever lives there is friendly and will let us come in to warm up."

As you draw near, the ghostly candlelight illuminates the figure. It is a man . . . and his face is extremely eerie. With dark shadows flickering over it, he looks like a monster.

"I'm not going in there!" Rodney sputters. "I don't care how miserable it is out here."

The three of you look at each other, worry all over your faces. Finally you decide.

"We have to check it out. If we don't we'll freeze to death." And with that you lead the way to the cottage.

As you approach the rustic little place, the door opens, and an old man with long, white hair peers out.

"Who's there?" he asks, still holding the candle. "What do you want?"

You tell him who you are and that you are lost. "Please, sir," you plead, your teeth beginning to chatter. "It's awfully cold out here. May we come in?"

"Of course," he says, standing back from the door and motioning you inside the small cottage.

The place is small and the furniture is crude, but

Turn to the next page.

it is warm and pleasant. Logs crackle and blaze in a large fireplace that dominates the room. Over the fire a pot is suspended and something is cooking, filling the room with delicious smells. On the mantelpiece is an ornate, old-fashioned clock.

The old man seems to be delighted to have company. In a long, brown woolen robe he bustles about and pulls wooden chairs near the fireplace. He tells you to sit by the fire, then brings you rags to wipe yourselves dry and blankets to put over your shoulders.

"Do you fancy a bit of nice hot soup?" he asks.

"Yes, please," the three of you say in unison.

The old man smiles as he ladles soup into wooden bowls and hands one to each of you along with a wooden spoon.

As you eat heartily, you look around the cottage. Simple drawings of trains hang everywhere. You wonder how that is possible, since you are in the Middle Ages and trains have not yet been invented.

"Sir," you ask the old man, "where did you get all these drawings?"

He sits down on a chair opposite you, a somewhat troubled expression on his face.

"I drew them," he says.

You continue studying the drawings. All seem to be of the same train, and it is on tracks.

Turn to the next page.

"I draw pictures of this thing, but I don't know what it is," the old man explains. "You see, I often have dreams in which this thing appears. Last night I had the strangest dream of all. It wasn't a dream really; it was more like a nightmare. There was a thunderous noise, a blinding light, and the earth moved. And then I woke up."

"How interesting," you say. "You're drawing pictures of something that hasn't been inv—"

"I have a theory," interrupts the old man. "I believe the dreams—and the pictures—are a prophecy, a revelation of a thing that will be coming."

"It's a train, sir," Elise tells him. "That's what they're called."

"Looks like the new Essex-Star line," adds Rodney. "It passes into Devon, probably through the area about where we are now. In fact, they just finished laying the track for it a few years ago." He laughs. "That is, a few years ago when we're not in this weird dream."

The old man gives the three of you a puzzled look. "What is all this you speak of?" he asks.

Rodney launches into a long, fumbling answer. He seems to be on the verge of telling the old man that you are from the future when Elise points out the window.

Turn to the next page.

"Oh, look," she says. "It's quit raining!"

"Indeed it has," says the old man, his attention diverted from Rodney's story.

But you are not looking out the window. You are staring in amazement at the clock on the mantelpiece. The hands are spinning clockwise, ticking off hours by the second.

"What's wrong with your clock, sir?" you ask.

"I've never seen such a thing!" the old man exclaims, as the hands of the clock begin whirling even faster. They are now nothing but a blur.

"What's it doing?" asks Rodney, an edge of fear to his voice.

"It's like we're going from the past to the future!" Elise exclaims. "Like racing from medieval times into the pre—"

Suddenly a shrieking whistle blasts, mixed with an ominous hooting and chugging.

You, your cousins, and the old man rush to the window. Puzzled, you stare at railroad tracks leading right to the cottage. Disbelief turns to horror as you see a train—the one in the pictures—come rumbling around a bend. Within an instant the mammoth locomotive, whistle wailing, is barreling directly at the cottage.

You do not even have time to scream.

Turn to the next page.

A thunderous roar fills the room. The clock hands spin furiously, and for a fraction of a second you glimpse the towering iron face of the locomotive, see its huge churning wheels—just before it slams into the cottage, shattering it into a million pieces.

"The gate's too risky. I'm afraid we'd never make it there without being spotted," you tell your cousins. "Let's see if we can find some other way out."

Walking in the shadows, the three of you continue down the alleyway and eventually make your way between a series of hovellike stone buildings. You turn a corner—and your heart almost stops as you run into a stout, towheaded young man.

"Ah, who have we here?" he says, backing the three of you into a corner. "You're the ones that everybody's lookin' for, aren't you?"

"Please don't turn us in," you beg.

"It could be my neck if I don't," says the young man. And then a gleam comes into his eye. "But if you were to give me all your gold I might be willing to let you go . . . maybe even help you."

"But we have no gold," says Rodney.

"No gold! Then you have nothing to offer."

A thought comes to you. You *do* have one thing you might trade—your watch. Should you tell him about it? Your parents gave it to you, engraved with your initials. But if you don't give it to him, he might turn you in.

If you choose to offer him the watch,
turn to the next page.

If you choose not to,
turn to page 48.

—"I *do* have something to offer you," you tell him, slipping your watch from your wrist.

"What is that?" he asks, not taking it from your outstretched hand. "It looks like a tiny clock."

You think quickly, trying to come up with some sort of explanation as to how and why you could have such a thing in the Middle Ages. "It is, and it's very rare," you say. "You see, large clocks are common, but in a far-off land I bought this magical, tiny clock." You offer the watch to the man again. "Here, take a closer look."

This time the man takes the watch and examines it with great interest. "You say it goes here?" he asks, pointing to his wrist.

"Yes," you say, and seeing that the man has trouble putting it on, you help him. "Now will you help us?" you ask, seeing how the man is eyeing his new possession with obvious pride.

The man nods and takes off down a winding path. On his heels, you follow him to the castle wall. Behind a stable is a heavy iron gate.

"This is used for taking the animals to and from pasture," says the young man, sliding back a heavy bolt and pulling the gate open. "Head across the meadow, then through the woods. Good luck," he says and gives you a wink as you hurry into the meadow.

Turn to the next page.

"Thanks," you call over your shoulder. "Enjoy the watch!"

You are not very far out when you hear loud voices and footfalls behind you. Immediately you lie flat on the ground, trembling as you hear the young man shouting at soldiers who are shouting at him. Then the young man is pleading for his life. He screams, then screams again.

"We've got to help him," says Elise.

"But how?" asks Rodney. "We're the ones they're after."

From where you are hiding, you watch as a club-wielding soldier delivers a blow to the young man. Hurt, he staggers through the gate, then falls face first to the ground.

You feel sickened by what you've just seen, and also guilty, but there is no time to think about what just happened. Already soldiers are coming through the gate, searching for you. Jumping up, you run wildly for the dark woods.

Suddenly something catches your foot, and you fall . . . not onto the ground, but onto the floor in your bedroom at Aunt Cora's. You shake yourself awake, and find you have fallen out of bed, your foot tangled in the sheets.

You sit up, and for a long moment you think

Turn to the next page.

about your dream of being in Ormonde Castle back in the 14th century. The grisly killing of the young man is the part of your dream that troubles you the most.

Slowly you pick yourself up and go to the window. Faint rays of sunlight illuminate a cold, early-morning fog. You dress hurriedly and make your way downstairs. No one except Rodney is up yet. He's about to leave through the back door.

"Going for a walk," he says. "Want to come along?"

"Sure. Why not?" you reply, thinking a walk will help you get over your bad dream. You grab your windbreaker and head out with him into the overcast, cool morning.

The clouds begin to clear as you make your way up along the coast. Soon you find yourself passing Ormonde Castle. Because your dream had seemed so real, you are relieved to find that the place is—as it should be—nothing but crumbled ruins. You think about telling Rodney about your dream, but decide against it.

Rodney heads up into a leaning, lichen-covered remnant of a tower. The place looks too dangerous to you so you set off alone, wandering around the ancient battlements, most of which lie in heaps.

Turn to the next page.

Crawling over the remains of a wall, you pick your way carefully down a short slope. Winded, you sit down to rest, but suddenly jerk back in revulsion. Part of a human skull sticks out from a jumble of rocks. You are tempted to run, but then begin to dig with your hands, tossing stones aside, unearthing more and more of the skull's skeletal body. You expose an arm bone and then a hand. From the bony wrist you remove the remains of a watch . . . with your initials on the back.

"No!" you gasp, goose bumps crawling up your spine. "It was just a *dream!*"

There's something about the young man you don't trust, so you decide it's best to hold on to your watch. "I wish we had something to give you," you say, "but—"

Angered, the young man doesn't wait for your excuse. He cups his hands to his mouth and yells for the guards.

You start to run away, but the young man is right on your heels. Out of the corner of your eye you see him snatch a fishing net someone had left hanging on a peg to dry. An instant later he tosses it over the three of you. Helpless, you lie in a tangled heap of arms and legs.

Within minutes, fearsome hulking forms loom into view. Momentarily you and your cousins are dragged roughly to your feet by helmeted soldiers in chain-mail tunics.

"Caught 'em, I did!" boasts the towheaded young man.

"Good lad!" rasps a towering, bearded soldier. He turns his attention to the three of you and to the other soldiers. "Untangle this mess," he says, laughing cruelly. "Then take these three fish to the dungeon."

Elise, half-conscious from the struggle, has to be carried. But Rodney continues to fight furiously and almost breaks free. For his trouble, his legs are tied

*Turn to the **next page**.*

and he is dragged along by two angry soldiers. Resigned to your fate, you walk quietly toward a door, prodded along by a single soldier.

The dungeon is deep in the back of the castle, down two flights of stone steps. It is a wretched, foul-smelling chamber about the size of an average basement.

Elise is dumped unceremoniously on the dank stone floor. She moans, frightening you and Rodney. Together you help her to sit up.

"What are you going to do to us?" you ask a soldier standing guard.

"Let Hulbert have his fun with ya," the soldier says simply. "Use the thumbscrews, he might. Or put ya on the rack." Elise has stopped moaning and is now crying.

"Or cut your fingers off," the soldier continues, as if enjoying scaring you. "One by one, till ya tell all."

"Tell all about *what?*" Rodney asks. "We don't know anything."

The soldier laughs. "Don't tell me you're spying here in Ormonde for nothing."

"But we aren't sp—" you start to say.

"Tell Hulbert!" the soldier bellows. "He'll be down to see you shortly."

And with that he stomps up the dungeon steps.

Turn to the next page.

He jangles some keys for a moment, then opens the heavy wooden door. "Spies who know nothing, ha!" the soldier sneers, then slams the door behind him.

Instantly the three of you are plunged into almost complete darkness. The only light source in the horrid chamber comes from a bit of frosty moonlight radiating from a barred window high overhead. Iron manacles and lengths of chain dangle from one wall. On the stone floor there are heaps of old, dirty straw, alive with roaches. These are supposed to be your beds. But this is nothing—for your eyes are riveted on an iron cage hanging from the ceiling. In it is a human skeleton, hands of bone gripping the bars.

"We're going to die in here," says Elise, almost matter-of-factly.

"But first we've got Hulbert to deal with," says Rodney.

"Yeah," you say. "And we'd better think of something to tell him." You begin pacing, examining the heavy door and single, barred window.

"There's no way out of here," Rodney says woefully.

"Are you sure?" asks a mellow voice.

Startled, the three of you turn in circles, looking for the source of the voice, and find yourselves staring at first a mouth, then a hand, then a body forming slowly out of thin air.

*Turn to the **next** page.*

"Don't be frightened," says the man who now stands fully formed in front of you. "I am Nuri."

"What do you want with us?" you stammer.

"You have a very, very interesting timepiece," says Nuri. "I wish to trade my timepiece for yours."

You look at your wrist, to where your watch is covered by your sleeve. You wonder how he knew your watch was there. You pull back the cloth of the sleeve, but there is nothing there. Looking to Nuri, you see your watch is already on *his* wrist, and in your hands is a large, circular metal disk with zodiac designs and a cranklike device on the face.

"What do I do with this?" you ask.

But as quickly as he appeared, Nuri is now gone.

Dumbfounded, you look down at the odd device.

"Maybe it will get us out of here," says Rodney, taking the thing from you.

"Be careful," says Elise. "We don't know what it can do."

But Rodney is already turning the crank backward. Suddenly night turns to day, then day to night, in rapid succession. Flesh covers the skeleton in the cage. It changes into a corpse, then becomes a live human being—a man in filthy, tattered clothes. Sitting up and gripping the bars, he screams, begging to be set free, his words coming out of him in reverse order.

Turn to the next page.

Then that prisoner disappears and another one appears—this one manacled to a wall. He, too, changes from a skeleton to a corpse to a live human. Now his hands are being forced into the manacles—but in reverse order—by soldiers, who then appear to back out of the dungeon with him.

"It's like a movie being rewound!" you exclaim. "Crank faster. Maybe you can crank us out of here!"

Rodney cranks as if his life depended on it.

A parade of reversed scenes unfolds before your eyes: a body with ugly red marks on it becomes a bug-eyed man being lashed with a leather strap; a female prisoner is eating from an almost empty tin plate that slowly fills with food; a man cries, "!this . . . do . . . Don't," to a soldier who laughs backward.

Suddenly you, Elise, and Rodney are out of the dungeon and back outside, tangled in the fishing net. Then you are out of the net and about to run away, when you stop short.

"Hey!" you yell. "We've gone so far back in time, the castle hasn't even been built yet."

"Do you think if we crank forward the castle will reappear?" Elise asks. "I don't want to go back in there."

"Yeah," you say, "but don't you want to return to the 20th century? Maybe if we crank fast enough

Turn to the next page.

we'll pass right through my nightmare and end up at home!" Without waiting for a reply, you turn to Rodney. "Crank us into the future!" you shout to him. "Crank forward as fast as you can!"

Once again Rodney cranks, but this time he cranks forward with everything he's got.

Instantly the landscape around you changes from fertile to fallow and back again as the years pass. The weather changes again and again, too. Suddenly the castle looks a lot older; its walls are now grime covered, darkened with age, eroded and weakened by the passing of the centuries.

As the whole place begins shaking, you realize in horror what is happening.

"Slow down!" you yell at Rodney.

But already it is too late. The walls of the castle collapse around you, and the three of you are crushed . . . buried . . . and swallowed up in the present-day ruins of Ormonde Castle.

"Upstairs!" you yell to your cousins.

Taking the steps two and three at a time, you race upward. Rodney and Elise are right behind you.

With the soldiers in hot pursuit, you come to a landing. To your right is a door and you smell a stench coming from behind it. Directly ahead are steep, narrow stairs that wind upward, disappearing into total blackness.

Neither way looks appealing, but the soldiers are almost upon you.

If you decide to go through the door,
*turn to the **next page**.*

If you head up the narrow stairs
through the darkness,
*turn to **page 61**.*

You push open the door, and the foul odor nearly knocks you over. What is worse is the horrible
moaning and weeping. You take a few apprehensive
steps into the semi-dark of a large room, then feel
nauseated at the sight before your eyes. All around
on crude wooden beds and pallets on the floor are
men, women, and children. They are terribly ill and
groaning in pain, their emaciated bodies covered
with lumps and ugly, dark blotches. Dark, sunken
eyes follow your every movement.

Fearful and sickened, you and your cousins back
away, then turn and hurry toward the door. But you
stop in your tracks the second you swing it open.
Just outside soldiers, weapons in hand, loom into
view. But they aren't pushing you back in. Instead,
they just stand there, smiling cruelly.

"They're in with them what's got the plague!"
yells one of the soldiers in a booming voice.

"Then let 'em die in there," another says, laughing as he pulls the door shut with a bang.

You, Elise, and Rodney cower in a corner not knowing what to do. Outside you hear something slammed
against the door, then the sound of hammering.

"They're boarding up the door!" cries Rodney.
His head swivels and his eyes fix on the plague victims. "We're going to die just like them!"

Turn to the next page.

Tentatively the three of you make your way through the room of sick people. There are at least two dozen of them, and about a half-dozen corpses are piled in a corner.

A young man, his face pale and sunken, sits on a high-backed chair. He wears a cone-shaped hat and a robe with an odd, geometric design.

Hanging from his neck is a triangular piece of jewelry, the metal wrought into letters that repeatedly form the word *abracadabra*. Gazing at you with feverish eyes, he pulls a filthy blanket over his shoulders. "Who are you?" he asks, his voice a coarse whisper.

You are too terrified to answer.

"You don't look sick," the man says. "What are you doing here in this place of death?"

"The soldiers locked us in," you explain.

"And sentenced you to your doom, they did." He extends a waxy-looking hand. "Me name's Edric." He chuckles knowingly when he sees that you and your cousins are too afraid, and too repulsed, to take his hand.

The laughter becomes louder, stronger, and you gaze in disbelief as he removes the skin from his extended hand. It slips off, all in one piece, like a horrid glove.

Turn to the next page.

Rodney vomits, which just sets Edric laughing again.

The laugh now is peculiar and seems laced with evil. "There are greater horrors than death," he says, removing a glove of skin from his other hand and placing it beside the other on the floor. They look like a surgeon's rubber gloves, ready to be put back on when needed.

"What you did with your hands—it's not possible," you say to Edric, your mind reeling.

"All things are possible," Edric replies. He picks up a very small wooden box from the floor and places it in his lap. He opens its cagelike door and out flies a dove.

You watch as it circles the room several times, then makes a fluttering landing on Edric's shoulder. You step closer, gaping in disbelief at what you see. The dove has a human face.

"All things are possible," says the dove.

"We've got to get out of here!" gasps Rodney.

You agree, but looking around the room you see no window or door to escape from.

Edric smiles as more doves with human heads fly out of the box. First you count three, then five or six more, then out flutter countless birds, hundreds of them emerging in an unending stream, all from the

Turn to the next page.

single tiny box. The room fills with them and the noise of their flapping wings.

Edric puts on his gloves of skin and claps his hands together. Suddenly all the doves stop in midair and midflight. They shrink down to the size of dots, then vanish altogether.

"That abracadabra thing hanging from your neck," says Elise nervously. "You're a magician, aren't you?"

Edric nods proudly as a girl on a straw pallet beside him rises to one elbow. She looks up at you and your cousins. "Edric's magic is true," she says. "It is the magic of life and death."

"Do not listen to her," Edric says firmly.

A hurt expression on her face, the girl lies back down and closes her eyes.

"No one listens to her anymore," Edric goes on. "She's dead."

"She's not dead," Rodney protests. "She just spoke to us and moved and—"

Edric spits a needle from his mouth. He plucks it from the air, then pokes the girl in the arm with it. "See," he says, "she doesn't feel a thing."

"What's going on in here?" stammers Rodney. "I don't even know who's alive and who's dead!"

"Please," you beg. "How do we get out of here?"

Edric grins, points at the dead girl beside him,

Turn to the next page.

then in the direction of the corpses piled near the far wall. "As they did," he explains. "Death is the only exit from this room."

"But not for us!" exclaims Elise. "We're not even sick!"

Edric smiles cryptically, then snaps his fingers.

Instantly Rodney coughs. He crawls on hands and knees, hacking uncontrollably. At the same time Elise begins to cry, rocking back and forth, holding her stomach. You feel sick, too. Your head is spinning, and you break into a cold sweat.

Suddenly you hear a creaking coming from outside. Then you hear a plaintive wail, "Bring out your dead!"

Edric raises his hand and a window magically appears.

You stumble to it. Looking out, you see the town within the city walls. Corpses lie in the streets and outside of homes, each of which has a red mark painted on the door.

Down the street comes a horse-drawn wagon filled with more plague victims, followed by men carrying torches. "Bring out your dead!" calls the driver.

You turn and are aghast to see Elise and Rodney in motionless heaps on the floor. You stumble to them, kneeling down to gaze into their lifeless eyes.

Turn to the next page.

"My cousins!" you cry. "They're dead!"

Edric laughs. "And now it is your turn!" Grinning menacingly, he snaps his fingers.

It is as though he has snapped the thread of life within you. All goes black. You feel yourself topple over onto your cousins . . . but in the same instant, even as you die you float upward . . . and find yourself hovering above your own body.

Edric stands and spreads his arms. "It's time!" he bellows.

The dead girl opens her eyes and stands up. One by one, the corpses in the corner untangle themselves and get to their feet—as does your own corpse, and those of Rodney and Elise. Suddenly a door appears in the wall.

"Come, everyone," says Edric, leading a band of zombies toward the door. "Come!" he commands even louder, as the corpses follow him out of the place.

You hear the horse-drawn cart coming down the street. "Bring out your dead!" the driver calls woefully. "Bring out your dead!"

Groping your way in total darkness, you head up the stairs that wind in a tight spiral. Finally, above and ahead, you see a light and you find that the stairs lead directly into a room. It looks like a bedroom of sorts, round in shape and seemingly the topmost part of a tower.

A young, pretty girl with long, black hair is seated at a table doing needlepoint. Seeming not at all surprised by your sudden appearance, she looks up and smiles at the three of you.

"Hello," she says in a pleasant voice. "I am Bridget. And you?"

Nervously looking over your shoulder at the sound of footsteps in the dark stairwell, you tell her your name and those of your cousins.

"And are the soldiers after you?" asks Bridget simply.

"Yes," says Elise. "And we haven't done anything. Please, can you help us?"

"Why, you are in the perfect room for that," the dark-haired girl replies.

"What do you mean?" Rodney asks.

"You're in the Changing Room," she replies matter-of-factly. "It is the room in which wonderful things can happen. It is a—"

But you can hear the soldiers charging up the

Turn to the next page.

stairs, and in a panic you cut off her explanation. "Please, Bridget. Hide us!"

Bridget smiles calmly, radiating compassion and full understanding of your predicament. "No need to worry," she says, and snaps her fingers.

Suddenly Rodney is a mouse cowering in a corner, Elise is a figurine on the table, and you are a black-and-white kitten. As the soldiers storm into the room, you leap nimbly into Bridget's lap and begin to purr.

"Is something wrong, gentlemen?" she asks, stroking your furry coat.

The soldiers are staring about in confusion. "Has no one come this way?" demands the tallest soldier, apparently the leader.

"It would appear not, sir," says Bridget. "As you can see, I'm all alone."

Grumbling, the soldiers hurry back down the stairs.

Bridget continues to gently stroke your fur. You want to thank her for saving you, but you can form no words, only meows. The figurine of Elise on the table also seems to be trying to speak—with even less success than you. Rodney just squeaks as he peeks out from behind a chair.

Please change us back now, you beg Bridget with

Turn to the next page.

your thoughts. But, humming softly, she continues simply to pet you.

You see her soft, pretty hands. Then you are startled as they change into very old hands, laced with long, wormlike blue veins. You look up into her once pretty face, now a web of wrinkles. Her mouth is puckered, her teeth black and rotten, her breath foul. Frightened, you jump from her lap and, with your fur rising on your back, you hiss at her. She cackles, hacks, and wipes a bit of yellow spittle from her lips while you leap onto the table, accidentally knocking over the figurine of Elise. To your horror it falls to the floor and shatters. Dazed, you stare at the cracked and broken pieces of your cousin.

"Bad kitty!" screeches Bridget, and with a swipe of her hand, she knocks you off the table.

Landing on your feet, you hiss at her again . . . and then you smell something. It's a mouse! your cat senses tell you. Before you remember it is your cousin Rodney, in one fluid movement you are across the room and pouncing on him. Quickly you pin him to the ground and, with claws outstretched, tear into him as he squeals and squeaks frantically. You shake his mouse body back and forth. Then you eat him, carefully spitting out his tiny bones.

Your meal finished, you sniff around the broken

Turn to the next page.

pieces of the figurine, then easily leap back onto the table to clean yourself.

Bridget curses at you and tries to hit you with a book. But you are too quick. You leap from the table and dart down the stairs.

But the minute you leave the Changing Room, you turn back into a human, and the disgusting truth of what you did as a cat rushes back to you. Wailing with grief you descend the stairwell, which becomes blacker than the darkest ink. No longer possessing catlike senses, you become disoriented in the dark, and lose your sense of direction . . . and your balance. You trip, then tumble down the stairs knocking yourself out cold.

You awaken on the floor of the living room of Aunt Cora's house, at the foot of the staircase. Next to you is an overturned side table, and on the floor is a shattered figurine.

"My goodness!" your aunt exclaims, coming toward you in her wheelchair. "Are you all right, dear?"

"Yes," you mutter, stumbling to your feet, more embarrassed than hurt. "I'm so sorry. It looks like I've broken your figurine." Your heart is pounding as you remember your dream. You are too frightened to ask your aunt anything more about the broken piece.

Turn to the next page.

"Oh, don't worry about that, dear," Aunt Cora offers anyway. "Elise doesn't need a silly figurine. It's you I'm worried about."

"It—it was hers?" you stammer, about to faint as a mouse scurries by.

"Why, yes," Aunt Cora says, bending down to pick up a tiny porcelain face. She holds it up to the light. "Don't you think it bears an amazing resemblance to Elise?"

"This way!" you yell, heading down torch-lit stairs that corkscrew in ever-widening circles. The clatter of many footfalls are close behind, and, glancing back for an instant, you glimpse several soldiers rounding a turn above. One is hefting an ax, which he is about to let fly.

"Watch out!" you yell as the ax clangs against a wall, then skitters harmlessly past your feet.

The torches are set at an angle in stands in the wall, which sparks an idea. As you run by the next one, you grab it. Then you grab the next and the next, extinguishing each on the ground.

"What're you doing?" Rodney cries.

"Don't you see?" Elise asks, putting a torch out herself. "We're cutting off their light source."

Behind you the soldiers are plunged into blackness. You can hear them cursing and stumbling into one another as they feebly make their way down the dark stairs.

You hand one of the torches to Rodney, who hurries on with it at arm's length. Then you and Elise each take a torch and continue, around and around the downward-spiraling stairwell.

Finally you reach the bottom and enter a long, stone corridor. Stopping only now and then to pull a torch from the wall, toss it to the ground, and stomp

Turn to the next page.

out the flame, you race on.

Ahead a heavy wooden door comes into view.

Elise is the first to reach it. "Please, don't let it be locked," she pants, fumbling with the latch.

For a moment the door seems stuck, but the three of you lunge against it, and finally it swings open. Rushing through, you quickly bolt it from the other side and hurry away to the sound of fists beating on the other side of it. Then comes the sound of something heavier hitting it. Luckily the door is thick; hopefully the soldiers will have a hard time beating it down.

Your footsteps echo in the dank, seemingly endless underground corridor. Where does it lead? you wonder, noticing that your footsteps make a different sound now and then. Lowering your torch, you see you are walking over metal disks of rusty iron, similar to manhole covers but a bit smaller. The three of you stop. Studying one of the things, you find an inset ring-latch.

"What are these?" you ask, getting down on your knees.

The others follow suit and together you grab hold of the ring-latch. Pulling on it with all your might, you manage to raise the cover and drag it onto the stone floor.

Turn to the next page.

You aim your torch downward and in the flickering light see a narrow, rounded, rock-lined shaft. Thick, rusted rungs—footholds and handholds—disappear downward into the darkness. Taking a deep breath, Elise heads down first to check it out.

After a few moments, her voice echoes from below. "I've reached bottom!" she yells. "There's a stone door directly ahead, and to my right is some kind of hallway. It's small," she adds, "and we'll probably have to crawl through it. I think I can get the door open by myself. Do you want me to check it out, or are we just going to take the crawl space?"

If you tell Elise to open the door,
turn to the next page.

If you decide the crawl space is best,
turn to page 72.

"The door," says Rodney, "might be a secret passageway out to the beach, but—"

"Open the door, then!" you yell down to Elise. "Sounds like the best bet."

"But . . ." Rodney attempts to finish his sentence. "Elise, no! If it's high tide—!"

And from below the sound of the stone door squealing open is already being drowned out by the groan of rushing water. Screams from Elise turn into sputtering gurgles. Then they are completely drowned out by a thunderous swish and splash of water filling the tunnel.

"Elise!" you and Rodney scream, but there is no answer.

Crying, Rodney climbs partway down the shaft and aims his torch below. You catch a glimpse of a hand—Elise's—just before it is sucked under a huge gush of water.

"Elise!" you cry over and over again. *"Elise!"*

And then you sit up in bed—in Aunt Cora's house.

Haunted by the horrible, vivid image of your nightmare, you try to calm down. It is still dark out, and glancing at the clock you see that it is only a little after six-thirty in the morning. Still, there seems to be a lot of commotion in the house. Voices waft up from

Turn to the next page.

below, and you realize that the voices are probably what woke you.

Dressing quickly, you hurry downstairs. You hear a voice from the kitchen, then someone hangs up a phone. The voices become clearer—someone is crying.

"Good morning," you say tentatively as you enter the kitchen.

Your dad looks sorrowfully at you and you see that Rodney has been crying. Aunt Cora looks away, out the window, and wipes tears from her eyes as well.

"What's wrong?" you ask. "Why didn't anyone wake me up?"

"We tried, but you were dead asleep," says your father, sighing heavily. "We don't know what happened," he continues. "We don't understand it, but this morning, when Aunt Cora went to awaken Elise, she—" He clears his throat noisily. "She was—"

"The coroner," Rodney blurts out, "took Elise away an hour ago. She's dead!"

"What!?" Your heart is already racing, remembering your dream. "What . . . what did she die from?"

Aunt Cora stifles a sob.

"That's what we don't understand at all," your father says. "She was all bruised and battered, soaking wet, and—"

"No!" you cry. "It's not possible. It's like in my—"

Turn to the next page.

"Elise," Aunt Cora interrupts, "died in bed. But we just got a call from the doctor who examined her." She bursts into tears again. "It just doesn't make any sense. He said the cause of death was drowning."

"Wait up!" you yell to Elise. "We haven't had much luck with what's behind closed doors. Rodney and I will come down and we'll take the crawl space."

You and Rodney make your way down the shaft. With you in the lead, the three of you crawl along the dark, undersized passageway. It is an awful place. Ahead in the darkness rats squeal, and the walls and low ceiling are crawling with snails and cockroaches. Everywhere there are horrid-smelling puddles, pockets of muck, slime, and algae, making your journey not only disgusting but slippery as well.

You come to a fork in the crawl space. You detect a bit of light and you hear sounds—human voices mixed with an occasional booming noise—coming from the fork to the left. All is silent down the right fork, and putting your torch ahead of you, you can see a number of dark, twisting turns.

"Left or right?" asks Elise.

If you take the left fork,
turn to the next page.

If you take the right fork,
turn to page 76.

"There are people to the left," you tell your cousins. "Maybe they can get us out of here."

Rodney grumbles at your decision, concerned that the noises you hear may signal danger of some kind, but grudgingly falls in line as you veer off to the left. It angles up, and the farther you go, the steeper the angle of ascent. As you proceed, the voices accelerate to screaming, and the occasional booming becomes louder and more frequent. But you've come too far to stop now.

Almost to the point of exhaustion, you finally reach the end of the left fork and are faced with a rope ladder that leads up to a trapdoor. You climb up, push it open, and one after the other, the three of you crawl into what appears to be a storage room for weapons and munitions. A few crossbows, lances, and swords are stacked in corners, and there are kegs and kegs of gunpowder.

Going to a slitlike window you peer out—and quickly understand what all the noise and commotion are about. The castle is under siege, and a ferocious battle is raging. Fusillades of arrows whistle through the air. Some of these have flaming tips, starting fires in many parts of the castle. At the main gate there is a relentless, booming thud. And with each thud, the gate bends inward. Already some of

Turn to the next page.

the hinges appear to be giving way and the heavy gate looks likely to crack soon.

In awe, the three of you watch soldiers on battlements heaving large stones down at the attackers. Others are tipping heavy cauldrons of boiling oil over the walls to the horror of the unsuspecting enemy below. At the same time other soldiers are firing longbows, crossbows, and large, clumsy-looking cannons.

As you watch, a knight in chain-mail screams, falling backward from the wall. He has been hit by an arrow.

You turn to your cousins. "Did you see that poor guy?" you ask.

But neither Rodney nor Elise is listening. Their attention is directed above. The roof of the room you are in is burning.

"We've got to get out of here!" Elise yells. "There's gunpowder in here, and if—"

Rodney doesn't hear the end of that sentence. He's already desperately pulling on the door, but it won't budge.

"The trapdoor!" you yell. "It's our only hope!"

Two walls are now completely ablaze. Putting your hand in front of your face, shielding it from the scorching flames, you try to make your way to the trapdoor. The room is already so hot you feel as if

Turn to the next page.

you are being cooked alive.

Suddenly the ceiling collapses, completely covering the trapdoor with burning rubble.

You scramble back, coughing and choking, to find refuge in a corner.

Meanwhile Rodney is screaming, kicking on the door and slamming it with his fists. Elise is frantically trying to force her way through the narrow slit of a window. Frustrated, she can get only an arm through and nothing more.

From your crouched position in the corner, you observe their attempts at escape are useless.

Suddenly there is a horrid cracking noise above them, and almost in the same instant, a huge, flaming beam gives way and collapses on them.

You listen to their tortured screams, knowing there is nothing you can do to help them . . . or yourself. All you can do is sit . . . and wait for the explosion . . . as you watch the flames lick around the kegs of gunpowder.

"Let's try the tunnel to the right," you suggest, as you crawl into it. As soon as you enter the narrow opening, it widens enough so that you can easily walk through it. The tunnel has an odd scent to it, almost like baby powder, mixed with a musty smell. It is unlike anything you've encountered so far.

Your torches lighting the way, you and your cousins follow what seems to be an endless series of twists and turns. Finally the tunnel straightens, and there are stone steps ahead. Climbing these, you find that the stairs lead to a brick wall. You run your hands over the wall, looking for any sort of way in. About to give up, your hand pushes on one brick, and as if it were a button, it causes the entire wall to turn inward.

Entering, you flip the wall closed and turn around to find yourselves in a richly decorated room. Large, beautiful tapestries hang from the walls. There are plush chairs and finely crafted tables adorned with silver candelabra and gold bowls.

On top of one table is a large, leather-bound book. Its cover is embossed and intricately gilded with the numbers *1307*. Taking up much of the room is a very large bed with a beautiful white lace canopy.

"This is a royal person's room," says Elise, awestruck. "Maybe it belongs to a king or queen."

Turn to the next page.

"We should get out of here!" says Rodney, his eyes fixed in the direction of a hallway leading out of the room.

"Well, I don't think I could move another inch," says Elise. "That bed sure looks inviting."

Your hand is on the thick, leather-bound book. You are tempted to open it, but like Elise you are also extremely tired. Your gaze drifts to the bed. To lie on it, if only for a moment, would be so wonderful.

If you decide to go down the hallway,
turn to the next page.

If you open the book,
turn to page 88.

If you risk lying down on the bed,
turn to page 90.

"Rodney's right," you say. "We'd better get out of here."

The three of you make your way quietly down the long hallway. Ahead and to your right you see a closed door of heavy oak. On tiptoes, not making a sound, you and your cousins try to pass the door without being noticed. Suddenly your hair stands on end.

"Come in!" a man's voice bellows from within.

The three of you freeze in your tracks and, looking up, spot a small speaker above the door.

"I know who you are," says a man's voice. "I know the young lady who is called Elise, as I do her brother, Rodney. But most of all I know the one who is the dreamer, the one whose nightmare this is."

You exchange glances with your cousins. Though you say nothing, you are all wondering the same things: Who is he? How does he know who you are? And since when do Medieval castles have speaker systems?

"You are seeking an exit from your dream," the voice continues through the speaker. "Perhaps that exit is in here, perhaps not. But you'll never know unless you enter . . . *if you dare.*"

*If you enter the door,
turn to the next page.*

*If you decide to continue down
the hallway, turn to page 86.*

"I'm going in," you tell your cousins. "If nothing else, I want to find out how he knows us."

Rodney and Elise agree, and you turn the latch. The door slowly creaks open, revealing *another* door. Though you don't touch it, the door slides open at your hand's approach, as if it has sensors of some kind.

"Welcome," says a man sitting behind a desk.

The room you are now in looks like an ultra-modern office, complete with wall-to-wall carpeting, electric light fixtures, a telephone, and the usual sort of contemporary office equipment—computer, photo-copier, fax machine, as well as quite a few high-tech items you have never seen before.

"Please," says the man, gesturing toward chairs and a small sofa in the room, "have a seat."

But the three of you remain standing, bewildered at finding a room such as this in a medieval castle. You are also transfixed by the appearance of the man behind the desk. He gives the impression of being a businessman—from the future. He is wearing a suit of a design you've never seen before, a high-collared shirt, and a very short, luminous tie.

"Whe-where are we?" Elise stammers.

Smiling, the man picks up a remote control, presses his thumb to a button, and the sliding door

Turn to the next page.

rolls closed behind you.

"Excuse me, sir," you say, more than a little alarmed, "but who are you and—?"

The man taps the nameplate on his desk, which reads DR. H. BALDWIN. "Henry Baldwin," he says proudly. "Associate vice-president of Dreams, Incorporated."

You have to laugh. "Dreams, Incorporated? What's that?"

"Don't laugh, you unbeliever. I'm in an important position and responsible for quite a variety of things."

You apologize but, still grinning, ask the man exactly what he does.

The man clears his throat importantly. "Well," he says, "for starters, I record dreams onto ordinary videocassettes for later viewing on television sets."

"Cool!" Rodney exclaims. "What else do you do?"

"We also make audio recordings of dream sounds—that way people get all the sights *and* the sounds of their dreams," the man continues, sounding exactly like a commercial. "We just came out with that new feature last year."

"What do you mean by 'last year'?" you ask.

Dr. Baldwin looks impatient. "Well, if this year is 2058, naturally I mean 2057," he replies, "which is,

Turn to the next page.

as I'm sure you readily see, about half a century after your time."

"Then you're from the future!" Elise declares.

"You guessed it," Dr. Baldwin says, grinning. "Now I'll bet you're wondering what I'm doing in the 14th century." Dr. Baldwin makes a steeple of his fingers and studies you. "Well," he says, "that, my friends, is a difficult question to answer, in that I am not *really* here."

"Huh?" you exclaim.

Dr. Baldwin smiles. "It is not really me you are seeing, my young friend. Rather, because you are sound asleep, what you are seeing is a projection of me into your mind."

"In other words, I am dreaming you?"

"Yes. But I am more than a dream. I am quite real. That is, what I am doing at this moment is putting myself into your thoughts—your dreams—as you sleep."

You wrinkle your brow, trying to understand.

"You see," he continues, "you are part of my experiment."

"Experiment?" you ask.

"Yes, and quite an exciting one. A number of years ago, here at Dreams, Incorporated, we were finally able to electro-neurologically enter and

Turn to the next page.

change the shape of someone's dream. But it always was a person from the present—*our* present, the year 2051. My idea, my project, was to enter the dream of someone from the past, and alter that person's dream. And as you can see, I chose *you* as the subject of my experiment. I have put myself in your dream as you sleep."

"But why me?" you ask.

Dr. Baldwin suddenly avoids your gaze, as though for some reason this question seems to bother him. He looks about, then his face brightens with a smile—a bit forced, it seems to you.

"Would you care to see something—something *very* interesting?" he asks you and your cousins. And without waiting for an answer, he again picks up his remote control and taps a button.

Instantly a wood panel slides open, revealing a large, three-dimensional television. On the screen, you see yourself asleep in your bed at Aunt Cora's house. Dr. Baldwin again taps the remote control, twice this time, and the screen divides into three pictures. In addition to yourself, you now see Elise asleep in her room and Rodney asleep in his.

"Isn't it fascinating to be able to view yourselves!?" exclaims Dr. Baldwin.

The three of you nod, unable to speak.

Turn to the next page.

"As you can see," Dr. Baldwin continues, pointing a finger at you, "*you* are the primary dreamer."

"And the two of you"—he points to Elise and Rodney—"are coming along for the ride. You see, I've connected your dream experiences directly into that of the primary dreamer. So in effect, all three of you are having the same dream."

"This is really neat stuff!" exclaims Rodney, his eyes glued to the TV screen. He sits down on a sofa. "Do you think we could have a video of our dream?"

"Well, the dream *is* being recorded," Dr. Baldwin says, raising his eyebrows.

"Really?" you ask. "Could you play it back for us?"

Dr. Baldwin glances at his watch. "Yes, I suppose that *is* possible. However, I'm afraid there isn't time."

"What do you mean?" asks Elise.

"I must get you back," he says, nervously glancing at his watch again. "I have to get you out of your dream now."

For whatever reason, it is clear the man has decided that the time has come for you to exit the dream. Quickly you ask him once again why he chose you as his primary dreamer.

"It's best you don't know," Dr. Baldwin says gravely.

Turn to the next page.

"What do you mean?" you ask, beginning to feel a bit apprehensive.

"Well," Dr. Baldwin begins hesitantly, "the president of Dreams, Incorporated who gave me the go-ahead on this project, was worried that the subjects of my experiment might tell others about our company and the sorts of things we do. That could cause problems. People might panic. They might investigate our work. They might even try to steal some of our plans. But the three of you were safe subjects because, well . . ."

A shock wave of fear hits you as you suddenly realize the only possible reason why you and your cousins, under the circumstances, would make appropriate subjects. You look at the TV and see yourself roll over in your sleep. The bed creaks, and at the same time a strange, high-pitched whining sound comes from the television speakers.

"I am *truly* sorry," says Dr. Baldwin, sadly. "But you were chosen because you will not have time to—"

His words are drowned out by the increasing volume of the piercing whine.

"You see, half a century ago"—Dr. Baldwin says, practically yelling now—"on this date"—he studies his watch—"twenty-six seconds from now, a 747 jetliner headed to Heathrow Airport lost power, fell

Turn to the next page.

from the sky, and—"

"—and crashed into Devon!" you cry. "We're all going to be—"

But you don't have time to finish your sentence. Nodding sadly, Dr. Baldwin pushes the remote control. . . .

In terror, you sit up in your bed in Aunt Cora's house. Looking around frantically, you hear Rodney yell something from across the hall. He is trying to be heard over the now thunderous whine directly overhead.

It is over quickly. You are knocked out of bed by the initial impact of the plane with the house, and for an instant you catch a glimpse of a jet engine tearing through the ceiling. You feel the house shudder, collapse, come apart . . . and then nothing, as the plane explodes—and every atom of your being disintegrates in a flash.

"Keep going," you tell your cousins. "I don't like the idea that this guy knows us."

The three of you hurry off down the hall. There are countless turns in it and you are beginning to think it will go on forever. Finally you come to what seems to be the end, but what a peculiar end it is. Ahead of you is an old-fashioned telephone booth— and the door is open, as if waiting for you.

"A *phone* in a medieval castle!?" exclaims Rodney. "They didn't invent the telephone until the 19th century."

"It sure is strange," Elise says, scratching her head. And then she nearly jumps into your arms when the phone actually rings. Not knowing what else to do, you peel Elise off of you and pick up the receiver.

"Hello?" you say.

The voice on the other end of the line is that of the man you heard when you passed by the door a while ago, but now it is a recording. You hold up the receiver so Elise and Rodney can hear, too.

"Thank you for calling Dreams, Incorporated," it says. *"If you'd like to return to the oak door, push 1 now. . . . If you'd like to call home, push 2 now. . . . If you'd like to go to the party, push 3 now. . . . If you'd like to know the truth, push 4 now. . . . If you'd like these choices repeated, press the star key."*

Turn to the next page.

"I guess we can try all of them," says Elise.

"Could be," says Rodney, "but which one do we try first?" He turns to you. "What's the verdict?"

You are puzzled. "Why does it always have to be *my* decision?"

Exasperated, your cousins look at you, then chorus, "Because it's *your* nightmare!"

If you push 1, turn to page 94.

If you push 2, turn to page 95.

If you push 3, turn to page 99.

If you push 4, turn to page 106.

Your curiosity gets the better of you. The old book looks so interesting. What harm could there be in taking a quick look inside?

Carefully you open the book and immediately recognize it as a diary, written in very old-fashioned English. Some of it is hard to read and understand—some of the words are spelled differently than you might spell them, and quite a few are clearly no longer used in modern times. One entry mentions a *geek*, who *"bitteth from chickens and other fowle their heads for the entertanement thereof of the people at carnivals and fares."* Continuing to flip through the book, you ponder the interesting and funny fact that the word *geek* once had such a different meaning from today.

You check out the last page. The entry reads: *21 August, 1307: On the morn, a thief was trapped abskonding with vittles and was summarily garroted by the soldier on watch at the direction of Lord Phelan. The invasion of Engla-land by the Norsemen continues and late on the eve, a feerse battle was fought and stemmed with the loss of many a fine knightes, whilst the barbarians were droven from the ramparts. Later a threesome of intruders of a young age were happened upon in the Queene Egidia's quarters. They were seezed and hanged from the gallows until deade by Lord Phelan.*

Turn to the next page.

"We've got to get out of here!" you shout. "This is a diary from the year 1307! And on the last page it says we're going to be found and hanged! It says—"

You stop short. Already it is too late. A nobleman with long hair, a pockmarked face, and a sword in hand, storms into the room with a half-dozen soldiers in tow.

"Seize them!" he orders. The three of you back away, then run. But it is to no avail. Strong arms grab you, Rodney, and Elise.

"Lord Phelan," asks a short, brawny soldier, "what shall we do with 'em?"

The pock-faced nobleman leers. "For intrudin' in the very chambers of the queen? Hang 'em, one an' all!"

"I have to get off my feet," you say, lying down on your side on the luxurious bed. Resting your head on a wonderfully soft goose-down pillow, you mumble, "I'll only rest for a minute." You sigh contentedly and smile at your reflection in a large mirror in a gilded frame across the room.

"But we can't hang around here," Rodney protests. "We'll get caught."

"Oh, relax," says Elise. "There's no one here."

Your two cousins begin to argue. You close your eyes—only for a second—but you feel yourself drifting off to sleep. You try to fight it. But you are *so* tired, and *so* comfortable. . . .

You awaken to total silence. Rodney and Elise are no longer arguing—and no longer in the room.

Rodney! Elise! a voice inside your head screams. Where are you? You try to cry out, but your lips won't move. In fact, you are paralyzed. You can hear, feel, and see—you are aware of everything around you—but you cannot move a muscle.

Someone enters the room. At first the person is out of your range of vision, because you cannot move your head or eyes. You hear a gasp, and then see a woman in a lavender gown hurry toward you. You watch her, your eyes fixed in an unblinking stare. She bends close and touches you with skinny fingers.

Turn to the next page.

"Your Highness!" she cries, then runs screaming from the room.

You lie in paralytic horror, waiting, listening, watching.

Your eyes fly to the mirror in the gilded frame. In disbelief, you see an old, ashen-faced corpse on the bed. There is no physical resemblance to you, but you realize in horror that the person on the bed is *you*.

Suddenly people are flooding into the room. An old man, his face a mass of deep wrinkles, bends over you and lifts your wrist.

"Dead!" he announces.

Exclamations of shock, followed by the sounds of weeping, fill the room.

No! you want to scream. I'm alive! And I am not who you think I am!

A man wearing a black robe looks down at you. "Rest in peace, Your Majesty." He puts his hands to your eyelids and closes them though one remains partly open so you can still see, if only slightly.

A sheet is pulled over you.

Come back! the voice in your head screams as you hear the sound of people leaving the room. Don't leave me!

Terror-filled minutes pass. Then an eternity of hours. Finally sunlight fills the room, brightening

Turn to the next page.

the sheet that covers you. You hear footsteps as people enter the room and gather about you. Then comes the sound of something heavy being put down on the floor. As the sheet is pulled back, you are seized with bone-chilling fear. Through your half-opened eye, you glimpse a wooden coffin.

Move! you command your body. Show them you're alive! You focus your attention on the index finger of your right hand, willing it to move.

But nothing happens.

Helpless, you feel your inert body being lifted and see the faces of the soldiers who carry you. And then your body is placed gently in the silk-padded coffin.

"Shall we close the lid?" someone asks.

"I think not yet," comes a response from a woman.

You feel yourself hoisted, and with your one paralyzed, nearly closed eye, you see the ceiling passing above as you are carried along corridors, then down stairs, and finally out into the light.

Next the sky, fleeced with clouds, comes into view, and you see the boughs of trees. All around, you hear weeping and smell incense. Then there's a jolt as the coffin is placed on the ground. You smell fresh dirt. Slowly a crowd of mourners gathers—among them, Rodney and Elise!

You want to call out to them. But it is impossible.

Turn to the next page.

Instead you concentrate again on moving the index finger of your right hand. Again nothing happens. Then suddenly you see the lid of the coffin closing.

Don't! you try to scream. Don't do this!

You hear the clatter of wood against wood as the lid is put in place. Instantly you are enclosed in darkness. Horror grips your heart as each nail is pounded in. The coffin is lowered into the grave, and you hear the thud of shovelfuls of dirt hitting the coffin.

And then it happens. Your right index finger moves! You begin to cry. No one can see it now!

Suddenly a knock on your coffin jolts you. "I'm alive!" you scream.

And then a blinding light snaps you out of your paralysis. You sit up . . . in bed at your Aunt Cora's house. You glance at the clock at your bedside. It is past eleven.

Elise has opened the blinds, filling the room with light. "Well," she says teasingly, "good morning, Your Highness! We thought you'd *never* wake up."

"I want to go back to the door with the speaker above it," says Elise. "Something tells me that room holds the key to a lot of answers about your weird dream."

"OK, let's give it a try," you say, and push 1.

Suddenly the phone disappears, and where it had been is the same door you had passed earlier.

Turn back to page 79.

"Let's call home!" Rodney and Elise exclaim.

"But does 'home' mean where *I* live, or does it mean where *you* live?" you ask them.

"Only one way to find out," says Elise. "Push 2."

You shrug and press the 2 on the phone.

Instantly you hear ringing on the other end of the line and then the phone being picked up.

"Daymore and Linden," says a woman. "How may I help you?"

Momentarily you are at a total loss for words. "I—I was trying to reach home," you stammer.

"Who are you?" the woman asks.

You tell her your name.

"Is this some sort of morbid joke?" asks the woman, sounding annoyed.

"No, ma'am," you reply. "I'm here with my cousins, Rodney and Elise Cullen, and we just want to go home—either mine or theirs."

You hear a sound like an angry gasp, and then silence.

"Ma'am? Are you still there?"

"I am going to hang up," the woman snaps. "I do not know who you are or what you are up to, but I do not like it one bit!"

"Please don't hang up!" you beg her.

"Hmm, perhaps you haven't heard the news." The

Turn to the next page.

woman's voice softens for a moment. "It *did* just happen, after all."

"What happened?" you ask, relieved to hear the woman becoming nicer, but afraid that what has happened might be something horrible.

"The names you gave me were of the three young people who were at Ormonde Castle," says the woman. "Is that correct?"

"Yes," you tell her. "My cousins and I are those three people."

"Well, I'm sorry to say that that is impossible," the woman says, a definite edge to her voice. "Those three youngsters are now in the next room."

You are flabbergasted by what you've just heard. "But how?" you ask. "How could they be there when we—" You stop yourself, your mind reeling. And then an idea comes to you. "May I speak to them, please?"

"I'm afraid that's impossible," the woman says, growing angry again.

"Why not?" you insist, and then jump as the woman slams the receiver down.

Baffled you slowly hang up. Your cousins are watching you.

"What happened?" asks Rodney.

"Who did you talk to?" asks Elise.

Turn to the next page.

You frown. "Some strange woman who says we were found at Ormonde Castle. And get this! She said we're now at some place called"—you stop to think back for a moment—"a place called Daymore and Linden."

"No!" cries Rodney, the color draining from his face.

"What happened?" says Elise. There is horror in her eyes. "Something happened to us."

You are totally puzzled. "What's wrong?" you ask them.

"Daymore and Linden," says Rodney, ghostly pale, his eyes locked on you, "is a funeral home in Devon."

Elise furrows her brow. "This doesn't make any sense," she says.

"Sure doesn't," you add, "but let's get out of here, anyway." The three of you head down a hallway. You come to a door, push it open, and gape in surprise.

You are on a paved road outside Ormonde Castle, which has returned to its battered, moldering state. It is late afternoon, and you are wearing the clothes you wore *yesterday,* when you hiked from Devon with your cousins up to see the place for the first time.

"Hey, something's wrong," Rodney says, looking

Turn to the next page.

at his wristwatch. "My watch has yesterday's date, and I'm wearing the same shirt I wore yest—"

A scream from Elise stops him. You turn . . . as a horn blares . . . and tires screech. . . . A tour bus, rounding a bend in the road, goes into a skid—and the back of it swings around—straight at the three of you.

"Let's see what the party's all about," you say, as you push 3. "It's about time we had a little *fuuuuuuuuun!*" You scream suddenly as a rectangular section of floor drops open beneath the three of you, shooting your group down a long wooden slide. You land in a heap in a sparse room. A man wearing a grotesque mask sits at the end of a long table.

"Are you here for the party?" he asks.

"I guess," you say, catching your breath, "but where is it?"

"Here," says the man, sweeping his hand grandly around the room. "And now that you've arrived, we have just enough people!"

The odd statement troubles you, and so does the man's hideous mask. Made of some sort of shiny material and tied behind his head with a ribbon, it consists of half a dozen or more eyes and mouths, in no particular pattern.

"Party time!" the man yells, his voice muffled behind the mask. He gestures to chairs around the table. "Please," he says, "have a seat."

Totally baffled, you and your cousins hesitantly sit down in hard-backed chairs. In front of each of you is a mask, and also what appears to be a party favor, a little cloth bag tied with colorful ribbon.

"Well, put them on," the man commands, glee-

Turn to the next page.

fully pointing to the masks.

Your cousins look to you to take the lead. Your mask is that of a pig's face, all twisted and deformed with clumps of warts around the mouth and a turned-up nose. Rodney's is a scaly lizard's head, and Elise's is a bird with human teeth. You shrug and put on your mask, and your cousins follow suit.

"You look wonderful!" exclaims the man. "Let the party begin!" And with that, he picks up a hand-bell from the table and rings it happily.

An instant later, a woman wearing a clown outfit and carrying a handful of short swords bounds into the room. She bows, introduces herself, then immediately begins juggling the swords. She is smiling and completely confident, but she is the most awkward and inept juggler you've ever seen. At first you are tempted to laugh at her as she keeps dropping the swords. Your stifled giggles however turn to horror— as she lunges for one of the swords, catches it by the blades, and slashes her hand badly. Almost in the same instant, another sword pinwheels through the air, cutting her nose and then the back of her hand. Still the woman keeps smiling and continues to juggle, seemingly in no pain and oblivious to all her cuts.

The poor woman keeps on juggling, and with each movement sends blood spattering all over the room—

Turn to the next page.

and onto everyone in it.

"Great show!" Rodney whispers to you sarcastically.

"I think I'm going to be sick," says Elise, wiping a splotch of blood from her cheek.

"Bravo!" exclaims the man at the head of the table, clapping enthusiastically.

The juggler smiles, bows, and, leaving a trail of red droplets, darts merrily from the room.

Your host rings the bell again. "Service!" he bellows, then grins as a parade of servants enters from a side door. In the lead is a hunchbacked woman carrying a covered silver platter. Behind her, a man carries a silver pitcher and several cups.

"Ah!" exclaims your host. "Dinner is served. But where is the music?" He frowns. "We must have music!" He cups his hands to one of the mouths on his mask. "Musician, please!" he calls. "Come, merry music maker!"

In darts the bloodied juggler, a mandolin tucked under her arm.

"Play something pretty for our guests," he commands her.

The former juggler, smiling gaily, sits down cross-legged against a wall and with bloody hands begins strumming the mandolin.

Turn to the next page.

Meanwhile the hunchback has placed the silver platter in the center of the table. She lifts off the oval cover and reveals a gaudily frosted cake.

"Serve our guests first," orders your host. "And you, sir, pour them something to drink."

The servant with the silver pitcher sets a cup in front of each of you and pours a red punch.

Elise screams when something plops into her cup—a human eye!

You and Rodney look in your cups. There are eyeballs floating in both.

"Drink up!" says your host, taking a big swallow and chewing on the eye that was in his cup. "Ah, delicious!"

Already nauseated, you watch as the hunchback slices into the cake. Beneath the frosting are live snails and slugs all intertwined with slithering pink garden worms. On each of your plates the hunchback slops a wedge of the disgusting mess.

You don't expect us to eat this stuff! you want to scream, but afraid to offend your host, you say nothing and just stare at your plate.

Rodney averts his gaze and Elise puts her hand to her mouth. All you can do is continue to stare in disbelief. Then you push your plate away.

"Oh, my! Not hungry?" asks your host, talking

Turn to the next page.

with his mouth full, a worm dangling from his lips. "It's really quite wonderful," he proclaims, wiping a bit of slime from his upper lip with the back of his hand. "Sure you won't have some?"

"I think we'll pass," you say.

"Not even a taste?" he asks.

All three of you shake your heads vigorously.

He hangs his head, as though disappointed. "I'm sorry it's not to your liking."

"I'm sure it's good," you say, trying to be diplomatic, "but it's not the sort of thing we're used to."

The man sighs. "Well, at least open your party favors."

With trepidation, you untie the ribbon on the little cloth packet in front of you to find an ordinary-looking egg inside. Your cousins also open theirs. They, too, find eggs.

"Crack 'em open!" your host says heartily. "I guarantee you'll love what's inside."

The servants are hovering about the three of you, watching over your shoulders. Your host is also looking on expectantly, as is the poor woman with the mandolin.

Your hand shaking a little, you crack open the egg—showering the floor with colorful confetti. Everyone laughs, including you, relieved to find

Turn to the next page.

nothing more than tiny bits of paper in the egg. Rodney cracks his egg open and the same thing happens. Thinking her egg is also filled with harmless confetti, Elise cracks hers over Rodney's head—and raw egg splatters all over his hair, spilling down his reptile-masked face.

Everybody laughs . . . except Rodney.

"I've had enough!" he complains, reaching for his mask.

"Don't!" commands your host. *"Don't take off your mask!"* he says emphatically.

"Why not?" Rodney asks, slowly lowering his hands.

"Because you'll ruin my surprise."

"Wh-what surprise?" you stammer.

"Oh, all right," he says, clearly disappointed. He takes off his mask, revealing a face of many eyes and mouths. "Surprise!" he shouts gleefully.

Elise screams.

"Quite a good likeness," says one of the mouths on your host's face.

"Even if I do say so myself," says another of them. "Now take off yours."

Knowing what your fate is, you, Rodney, and Elise take off your masks, then gasp in horror at the sight of one another's faces. Elise's face is that of a

Turn to the next page.

bird with human teeth; Rodney's is a scaly reptile's face; and you touch your own face, not surprised to feel clusters of warts around a pig's snout.

"Why did you do this?" you cry.

"Because now the party never has to end!" your host exclaims. The room echoes with his horrible laughter. "Don't you see? Now you can be party animals . . . forever!"

"I could sure use a few answers," you say, pushing the number 4. Instantly there is a blinding flash of light so intense you have to shut your eyes. Upon opening them you find yourself alone heading down the stairs in Aunt Cora's house. It is the middle of the night, and you hear tapping and chipping sounds coming from somewhere below. The sounds seem to be beckoning you. You are frightened for you feel that some terrible truth—about you and your past—is about to be revealed.

The tapping and chipping grow louder, as you cross the living room picking your way carefully past the dark shapes of furniture. A trace of light emanates from the kitchen. Entering, you see the cellar door slightly ajar with light filtering up from below. You hear voices from down there. It is your father and Aunt Cora, and along with their low voices is the sound of metal striking masonry. A clattering sound, like rubble falling, stops the voices. And then your Aunt Cora hisses, "Quiet! You'll wake up the whole house!"

"They're all asleep," replies your father.

"Well, if anybody ever finds out about this . . ." your aunt warns.

"No one's going to find out, Cora," your father insists. "I'll be done quickly. Soon you'll rest easy."

Turn to the next page.

Very curious, you carefully push the door open a bit more and peer down the dark stairs. There at the bottom, lighted by a lantern, are your father and Aunt Cora. She is seated in an old chair, her crutches propped against it, and she is aiming the lantern on a brick wall where your father is hacking away with a small pickax. Already he has made a large opening.

"Almost through," he announces. "Then I'll wrap it up, drive it to Southeby, and drop it down a mine shaft, like you said. But you'll have to go with me. I'm not that familiar with English roads anymore."

"As long as we're back before sunup," says Aunt Cora.

Your father goes back to work, and with the sound of his hacking at the brick wall muffling your footsteps, you slowly make your way downstairs for a better look.

A step creaks.

"I heard something," says Aunt Cora, turning her head.

Holding your breath, you retreat into the shadows and press your body against a wall.

The hacking sound stops for a moment, as your father stops working to listen. "It was just your

Turn to the next page.

imagination, Cora," he says, going back to work. He swings the pickax hard, and a section of cracked brick wall collapses. "I'm through!" he announces. Taking the lantern from Aunt Cora, he crawls through an opening in the wall.

You crane your head to see better and are horrified by what unfolds before your eyes. Your father emerges through the gap in the brick wall—dragging a corpse, which is little more than a skeleton.

In a state of shock and no longer able to control yourself, you walk down the stairs—into plain view.

"Wow, it's more decomposed than I thought," says your father, carefully laying the horrible-smelling body on the floor.

But Aunt Cora is not listening to him. Open-mouthed, she is staring at you. Following her gaze, your father turns, and seeing you, his face becomes a mask of shock, fear, and guilt.

"Dad!" you gasp, reaching the bottom of the stairs. "What are you doing?"

"We—we thought it best you never knew," says Aunt Cora.

"Knew what?" you cry, moving woodenly toward your father, your eyes on the skeleton. Bits of rotted clothing hang from what remains of the torso and shoulders. Brown, desiccated skin is wrinkled up

Turn to the next page.

over the bones, and tufts of brown hair sprout from the skull.

"Who is that?" you ask, your voice trembling.

Your father and Aunt Cora exchange glances but say nothing.

"It's really why I—*we*—had to come to England," he explains. "You see, Aunt Cora, my sister, plans to—really, she *has* to sell this house."

"And we had to get rid of the body," your aunt adds. "We were afraid that the new owners might discover the false wall and—"

"You murdered someone!" you yell, not caring if you wake up Rodney and Elise. "Didn't you?"

"No," says your father, sitting down dejectedly. "It was an accident, but we were afraid people wouldn't believe us. I suppose we panicked. I was young, only twenty-four, and I had just started a new job—here in England—and I had you, just a toddler of three to think about, and—"

"And so you buried the person behind this wall?" you blurt. "And now you've come back to England to move the body?"

"Please, dear," says Aunt Cora, "you have to understand. It was just a stupid argument over something so silly we can't even remember what it was now. I lost my temper and struck out at him, and took a

Turn to the next page.

tumble down the stairs—*those* stairs." She gestures at the flight leading down into the cellar. "And I've been in a wheelchair ever since."

You stare at Aunt Cora, trying to make sense of what she's saying. No one had ever talked much about her accident. All you'd ever been told was that years ago she had taken a bad fall and had injured her spine. "But I still don't understand," you say, not allowing yourself to be diverted. "Whose body is that?"

Tears are welling up in your father's eyes. "I know it's hard for you to understand, but—"

"Does Mom know about this?"

Your father stares blank-faced at you. "Your— your mother is . . ."

Horror creeps up your spine. "My mother is at home. We took this trip to let her write her book. Right, Dad?"

Aunt Cora touches your hand. "Your mother was with me at the top of the stairs when I fell," she said softly. "She was trying to intervene between your father and me, and when I fell, so did she."

"No!" you scream. "My mother's at home. She—"

"Your *step*mother's at home," your father corrects you. "It—it was an accident," he mumbles, shaking his head. "And under the circumstances, Aunt Cora and I—"

Turn to the next page.

His voice trails off as you gape at him in disbelief.
Then slowly you let your gaze drift to your mother,
a moldering skeleton lying in a misshapen heap on a
dank cellar floor.

"To the door!" you yell, grabbing Elise by the arm and running with her as Rodney pulls it open.

A moment later the three of you find yourselves outside the castle.

Tethered to a tree, as though left there for you, are three horses. Do you dare take the horses? Or do you leave them, and take off running on foot?

*If you take the horses,
turn to the next page.*

*If you run away on foot,
turn to page 117.*

The temptation to take the horses is too great. The three of you untether the beautiful animals, which are already saddled, and climb on. Rodney chooses a black stallion, Elise takes a sorrel mare, and you pick a pure white colt.

To your left is a moonlit sea. Breakers pound and hiss on the sandy beach, which is reachable by a short trail down a grassy slope. Ahead and to your right is a vast meadow fringed in the far-off distance by a dark forest.

"Stop!" bellows a voice.

You go numb with fear, and glance over your shoulder to see soldiers pouring from the castle. An arrow zips past your face, and with a loud *thwang*, impales the branch of a tree. Your horse looks back at you with fear-filled eyes, as though he is asking you which way to run.

If you head toward the beach,
*turn to the **next page**.*

If you head off across the meadow,
*turn to **page 116**.*

"Head for the beach!" you shout, and the three of you whip your horses into a run, then gallop away.

Cool night air blasts your face as you race down the slope and out onto the broad beach, kicking sand up all around you. The vast, glistening sea looms before you. You try to turn your horse as it heads right for it, but it ignores your command, as do Rodney and Elise's horses, and heads straight for the water.

"No!" you cry. And then, just before you hit the water, you feel yourself rising as your beautiful white horse leaves the sea behind and runs skyward, on currents of air.

Elise and Rodney are right behind you, and their horses are also flying.

Both frightened and enthralled, you look down at the sea, now miles below. You then find yourself in the folds of a cloud, in cold mist, as the horses gallop on and upward.

You pass out of the cloud into frigid, black air. Your teeth chattering and your breath coming out in frosty gasps, you bury your head against your horse's neck, seeking warmth.

"I'm freezing to death!" you want to cry out, but your mouth won't move. It is frozen shut. Your skin freezes, too, cracking off and falling away from your

Turn to the next page.

body like large sheets of ice. Trembling violently, you hug your horse's soft white neck even tighter . . . and then you open your eyes . . . clutching not a white horse's neck but a white pillow. You roll over and drowsily gaze at an open window through which a bitter cold wind blows. It is so cold that sheets of ice have formed on the windows.

Shaking your head at how amazing your nightmare was, you notice for the first time that your fist is clenched tightly. Since your fingers are so cold, you practically have to pry them open. And when you do, you nearly fall out of bed. You have been clutching a piece of coarse white horsehair.

"Across the meadow!" you shout, whipping your horse into a run.

But no sooner are the words out of your mouth than arrows fill the air. One hits Rodney in his arm, then suddenly two skim Elise's shoulders. You see Elise go down, and her screams mix with yours— and with those of your horse as it rears back, an arrow in its flank. In terror you grab its mane as it whinnies and rises on its back legs, its forelegs pawing the air. You struggle with all your might to hold on. But it is futile, and you feel yourself falling backward from the horse . . . and land with a bang on the floor beside your bed.

Rubbing an aching elbow, you sit up. There is a knock, and then the door to the bedroom opens. Your father peers in.

"Gee whiz!" he exclaims, "are you all right?"

The horses being there seems just too convenient. What if they are a trap, you wonder, reasoning that you could be considered a thief for taking them and imprisoned or executed for the crime.

"Forget the horses!" you yell. "Run for it!"

Together the three of you dash into the night down a long, dusty trail. But soon you realize the soldiers have made a different decision.

Already you hear horses snorting and whinnying—lots of horses.

You glance over your shoulder—the soldiers are storming after you on powerful steeds. They will overtake you in minutes.

Quickly the three of you jump off the trail and crouch in the high grass. As you watch the mounted soldiers charge past you down the trail and into the night, you take a moment to breathe.

You know that it won't take long for the soldiers to realize what you've done.

"Let's go!" you whisper, as soon as your breathing somewhat returns to normal.

"Where?" Rodney and Elise whisper back.

You look around for a moment, then point toward a dark forest, diagonally across the meadow about five hundred feet away. "Over there," you tell them. "Come on!"

Turn to the next page.

But Rodney and Elise are frightened. It's night-time, and the forest looks doubly threatening.

"Look," you say, firmly looking at your cousins, "the soldiers will have a harder time finding us in there." You pause for a split second. "Now, are you with me or not?"

Rodney and Elise look at each other, then each nods solemnly.

Within a short time you are now leading your cousins through the dark misshapen trees that, sil-houetted by the night, look like the twisted, upside-down skeletons of long-dead animals. You plow on and on, your feet getting soaked by the soggy, leafy mold underfoot, your flesh scraped and scratched by the brambles and briars all around you.

Gradually, as night fades to day, faint rays of dawn pierce the forest; and soon as you trudge wearily along, all is brightened by streaks of gold, yellow, and orange sunlight filtering through the trees. Emerging from the forest, you come upon a broad stream. Bordered with colorful flowers, the water not only reflects a rainbow of purples, yellows, and reds, but it is actually multicolored.

"It's beautiful," says Elise.

"But weird," says Rodney.

You step closer to the water. You have to agree

Turn to the next page.

with both of them. The colors do make the water gorgeous, but there is something odd about the peaceful-looking stream.

"Let's look for a bridge—or some way to cross this thing," Rodney suggests.

"What for?" says Elise. "It looks shallow. We can wade across." She turns to you. "Can't we?"

If you wade across the stream,
turn to the next page.

If you look for some other way
to cross, turn to page 124.

"C'mon," you say, heading into the stream with Elise right after you. "Getting our feet wet isn't going to hurt us."

"Could be deeper than you think," Rodney warns.

You and Elise look back at him. He is standing on the bank, arms folded stubbornly across his chest, rooted to the spot.

Elise just shakes her head.

"Don't worry about him," you tell her. "Let's keep going. He'll catch up when he realizes this is the best way." And with that, the two of you hold hands and continue sloshing across the stream, leaving Rodney behind.

To your surprise, the deeper you go, the warmer the water becomes. In fact, it feels as though you're walking in a heated wading pool. There is also a delightful aroma in the air that seems to emanate from the colorful water, as though perfumed. But the footing is not solid, and both you and Elise have to struggle to keep your balance. It is as though you are walking on polished stones.

Waist-deep now, you gaze into the lilac-colored depths. At first you are unsure of what it is you see. Is it your imagination, or do you see bones? *Yes!* It is not polished stones you have been walking on but a streambed full of skulls, scapulas, and femurs! Elise,

Turn to the next page.

you can see, has not realized this yet. You are just about to share your fears with her when suddenly you become aware of something else—the perfume-like aroma is changing into a putrid stench.

Elise notices that immediately. "What is that horrid *smell?*" she complains, wrinkling up her nose in disgust.

You don't want to tell her what you think—that it is the sweet-rotten smell of death that is now becoming so strong you are nearly gagging.

Suddenly Elise slips on something. "It's a skull!" she yelps, peering into the water. "Let's get out of here!" she cries, splashing ahead, an expression of fear and revulsion on her face.

You slog along after her. But the bank seems to be getting farther away. You look back at Rodney. Though you have traveled no more than a few yards, he now seems to be miles away. His hands are cupped to his mouth, and he seems to be yelling something. But you cannot make out a word he is saying. The distance, plus the babbling and hissing of the water, are drowning him out.

Something more immediate, much more pressing has grabbed hold of your attention: The warm water, once pleasant, now seems to be hot—unbearably hot. It feels as if it also might have an acidlike quality.

Turn to the next page.

"My skin burns!" Elise screams.

Excruciating pain courses through your body, and you, too, are screaming. Your skin feels as though it is on fire. You are thrashing about wildly. The movement of your feet stirs up the bottom, and a skull, then an entire rib cage float to the surface. More bones bob up and float all around you. But you are in too much agony to care. You feel as though you're being boiled alive.

"I can't take it!" Elise shrieks, holding up an arm with blisters scattered on it.

You look at your own arms. They are also streaked and covered with large blisters.

"Help me!" gasps Elise, slogging toward you, reaching out to you with blister-covered hands.

You push her away, your face burning as she touches your neck, peeling off a piece of it.

"Stop!" you scream. "I can't help you!"

"I'm not asking you to help me," Elise says calmly, pulling away a wet washcloth from your neck and replacing it with another. "But it would help if you'd try to calm down. We've already called the doctor."

"Doctor?" you ask.

"Yes," says your father. "You developed quite a fever last night. Aunt Cora's calling the doctor, but Elise here has been up half the night cooling you

Turn to the next page.

down with washcloths."

"Am I going to be all right?" you ask. "I'm burning up."

"You're going to be fine," your dad assures you. "We think it's probably just an outbreak of chicken pox. That's why Rodney's staying away. He's never had them, but Elise, Aunt Cora, and I have." He laughs. "Just look at your arms. You're spotting up like a leopard!"

You look at your arms, which are streaked with red and covered with blisterlike sores from where you have been scratching.

"I've never seen water that looks like that," you say. "It could be dangerous. Let's find a bridge."

The three of you head up along the stream. Rounding a bend, you come upon a beautiful, flax-en-haired girl kneeling by the water. She is barefoot, wears a loose gown, and has a garland of flowers in her hair.

"Hello," you call as the three of you approach.

She looks up and smiles. "Greetings," she replies in a pleasant voice, an empty expression on her face.

You tell her your name and those of your cousins.

Seemingly uninterested, the girl turns her attention back to the stream. "I am Tiffany Lord," she says softly.

Tired, you and your cousins sit down on the grass next to her.

"The water is lovely, isn't it?" she says. "I wish it could last."

You and your cousins exchange puzzled glances. "What do you mean?" Elise asks.

But instead of answering her question, Tiffany begins to hum and scoops up a handful of water. She stares at it for a moment, then shows it to you. To your astonishment, the water has turned into a solid shape in the palm of her hand.

"How did you do that?" Rodney exclaims.

Turn to the next page.

Bemused and preoccupied, Tiffany stares at the solid block of water. It turns into a flower, then a butterfly.

"That was amazing!" you say, staring at the butterfly as it lifts out of Tiffany's hands and floats off into the breeze. "You're better than a magician."

"Thank you," says Tiffany softly, scooping up another handful of water. She doesn't look at you as she speaks. Her attention is on the water, which she pours back and forth from one hand to the other. "Why does it always have to end?" she asks sadly.

"Why does *what* always have to end?" you want to know.

She looks up at you with a smile on her delicate features. "You don't understand what I'm talking about, do you? None of you do."

The three of you shake your head.

"*They* must already leave," she says, turning the water into a wand. She points it at Elise and Rodney, who immediately begin to fade, then disappear.

"Bring them back!" you demand.

The wand retracts into the puddle of water it once was in Tiffany's hands. She spreads her fingers and the water becomes a pocket mirror, which she hands to you. "You, too, have changed," she says. "Look."

Turn to the next page.

You look in the pocket mirror . . . and see a complete stranger.

"What have you done to me?" you ask Tiffany, watching the words come from a mouth not your own.

"I did nothing," she replies simply.

"Please," you beg. "Tell me what's happening."

"I'm asleep," says Tiffany. "I'm dreaming this."

"No," you protest. "You've got it all backward. I'm the one who's dreaming. I—"

"Please," says Tiffany. "You'll have to go now. You see, you're just like all the other people and things in my dreams. You'll be gone when I wake up . . . moments from now."

Moments later, in an apartment in Mabeline, Kansas, an alarm clock rings next to the bed of Tiffany Lord. She rolls over, pushes off the alarm, then for a moment dimly recalls her dream. Her mind drifts, and she wishes in vain that her dream and the people in it, such as you, could somehow be real.

Just
when you
thought
it was safe
to fall
asleep . . .

... Watch out
for these
other

NIGHTMARES!
HOW WILL YOURS END?

titles:

CAVE OF FEAR

PLANET OF TERROR

VALLEY OF THE
SCREAMING STATUES